A PICTURE OF HORROR

Few laypeople understood that a negative contained far more detail than a print could ever show. For most people a negative was just a blur of lines and shadows. But as Herb bent over the negatives, with his loupe in hand, he was in position to see exactly what there was to see.

Oh, God.

Herb almost fainted.

Books by Christopher Pike

BURY ME DEEP
DIE SOFTLY
FALL INTO DARKNESS
FINAL FRIENDS: #1: THE PARTY
FINAL FRIENDS: #2: THE DANCE
FINAL FRIENDS: #3: THE GRADUATION
GIMME A KISS
LAST ACT
REMEMBER ME
SCAVENGER HUNT
SEE YOU LATER
SPELLBOUND
WHISPER OF DEATH
WITCH

Available from ARCHWAY Paperbacks

Christopher Pike

Die Softly

AN ARCHWAY PAPERBACK
Published by POCKET BOOKS
New York   London   Toronto   Sydney   Tokyo   Singapore

AN ARCHWAY PAPERBACK *Original*

 An Archway Paperback published by
POCKET BOOKS, a division of Simon & Schuster Inc.
1230 Avenue of the Americas, New York, NY 10020

ISBN: 0-671-69056-6

First Archway Paperback printing April 1991

10 9 8 7 6 5

AN ARCHWAY PAPERBACK and colophon are
registered trademarks of Simon & Schuster Inc.

Cover art by Brian Kotzky

Printed in the U.S.A.

IL 9+

FOR MIKE, MY BROTHER

PROLOGUE

In the End

Herb Trasker was dreaming when his mother knocked on his bedroom door to tell him a police sergeant was on the phone. Herb had received a call earlier that morning, so he had already been awakened once. The first call had been from a friend, and after talking to the friend, Herb had unplugged the phone in his room and gone back to sleep.

In his dream Herb and several of his friends were Old West pioneers, who were crossing a desert on horseback. The glaring sun was burning into the tops of their skulls. They were out of water. Two of their horses had died and the others were ready to drop. It was a hellish situation. Herb knew that the flies that buzzed around his face were just waiting till he could no longer brush them away.

They spotted a little shade beneath a dusty cliff and dismounted. While resting and trying to figure out where to look for water, another of their horses

1

collapsed. Everyone fell silent and stared stonily at one another. There were six of them: Herb's best friends, Sammie and Theo; Herb's favorite fantasy, Alexa; Alexa's boyfriend, Stephen; and Lisa, the head cheerleader at school. The fact that a girl whom he knew to be a cheerleader was part of an Old West expedition didn't seem unusual in the least.

One and all they sensed their doom closing in on them. There was no sign of shade across the wide parched plain, but then suddenly a huge black shadow like that of a giant Grim Reaper took shape far to the south. It was in the form of a dust cloud. They may have seen it with their eyes; they may have only sensed it in their hearts. In dreams it is often hard to tell the difference. In either case, something was coming out of the south, and it frightened them.

But what this thing turned out to be was Roger Corbin, Theo's brother. He came riding up on a white horse, and looked fresh, neither tired nor dusty. He had supplies with him, and his canteens were full. They accepted them gratefully, and Roger smiled at them as he dismounted. He wanted to know how they had gotten so lost.

"You're far south of Mannville," he said.

"How far south?" Herb asked. Mannville was home—it was where they had all grown up. That fact didn't strike them as unusual, either.

But something did trouble Herb. The water in Roger's canteen tasted good but it did nothing to quench his thirst. He took another gulp, and still another, without experiencing any satisfaction. It was as if his body were pricked with a million invisible holes that allowed the liquid to escape the instant he took it in. Or else the water was invisible, unreal, and he was only hallucinating that someone had come to their rescue. Also, Herb couldn't completely focus his eyes on Roger.

"Hundreds of miles south," Roger said. "You're in the middle of nowhere."

"How do we get out of here?" Theo asked.

Roger turned and stared at his brother. Sorrow touched his features. "Don't you know?" Roger asked.

"No."

Roger shook his head. "I don't know what to tell you."

"Do you have anything to eat?" Lisa asked. Lisa had been Roger's girlfriend—before. That was another odd thing—Herb couldn't remember why they had broken up, although he sensed it had been something important.

Roger brightened at the question. "I have cookies," he said.

Lisa smiled. "What kind of cookies?"

Roger reached for his saddlebag. "Your favorites."

"Great," Lisa said, taking gulp after gulp from the canteen. She, too, seemed to be having trouble satisfying her thirst.

They sat in the shade of the cliff and ate Roger's cookies. They were very sweet and only aggravated Herb's thirst—he took only a few crumbs. They tried to get Roger to tell them more about which direction they should head to get out of the desert, but his answers were vague. After a while Herb noticed that none of the flies were pestering Roger.

"Roger," Herb asked. "Where did you come from?"

Roger nodded south. "From that way."

"And what's out there?" Herb asked.

Roger gave him a long look. "Some say the edge of the world."

Herb chuckled. "Seriously."

Roger sat up and looked at his brother, Theo. "It's good to see you again, buddy," Roger said.

Theo became thoughtful, and lines creased his forehead. "I haven't seen you in a long time," Theo whispered.

"Yeah, you have," Herb said. "We saw Roger just the other— When did we see you last, Roger?"

Roger stood up suddenly. "I better be on my way."

Theo jumped up. "Wait. You just got here. I want to talk to you. I haven't talked to you in six months."

They all fell silent and thought about Theo's comment. It *was* true that none of them had spoken to Roger in six months. It was up to Herb to figure out why they hadn't. He knew the evidence must be right in front of him. The sun was shining directly onto Roger's forehead but there wasn't a drop of sweat on his skin. Indeed, the sun could have been shining right through him. For the first time Herb noticed that Roger cast no shadow on the ground.

"Roger," Herb said, getting up slowly. "Weren't you in a bad car accident a while back?" They were in the Old West but he knew about cars—and that, too, was OK.

Roger climbed on his horse and nodded gravely. "Yeah."

"You were killed," Theo said, paling.

Roger looked down at the parched, baked earth. "Yeah, I died all right."

"Then how can you be here if you're dead?" Lisa asked, sounding bitchy and frightened at the same time.

Roger flashed a brief grin at the question. He scanned the surrounding desolation. "You'd be better off asking why you're here," Roger said.

"What do you mean?" Theo asked.

In response Roger began to pull off his leather gloves. Like the rest of them, he was clad from head to toe in leather chaps, blue jeans, a long-sleeved shirt, and a dark cotton bandanna. Like them, all they could really see was his face.

Roger took off his right glove slowly, finger by finger. When he finished and held up his hand, Lisa let out a bloodcurdling scream.

His hand was nothing but bones. He was a skeleton.

"This desert just sucks the life out of you," Roger

5

said sadly, studying his bony fingers. Then he turned to Theo again. "But the desert isn't to blame. The desert's just a place."

Theo moved to his brother and grasped Roger's gloved hand. "How do we get out of here?" he asked anxiously.

"How did you get here?" Roger asked. "If you know that, you can get out." He studied the group. "Some of you, anyway."

"What's that supposed to mean?" Lisa asked, and now she sounded really scared, and not just because her old boyfriend had come back from the dead. She was worried about herself and stood shaking in her boots. Perhaps it was the rattling sound her legs made under her jeans that had her spooked.

"Take off your gloves, Lisa," Roger said.

Lisa took a step back. "No."

"Roll up the sleeves of your shirt," Roger said, showing no pity. "Go ahead, Lisa."

"No," she cried. "I'm not like you."

Stephen, who had so far remained silent, grabbed Lisa from behind. She screamed and tried to squirm free, but not before Stephen had ripped off one of her gloves. Then she screamed again, and this time couldn't stop.

Her hand had no flesh. It was nothing but bone.

"She's a monster," Stephen swore.

"Get her away from us," Sammie cried.

"Look at your own bodies," Roger said.

6

Stephen and Sammie backed hurriedly away from each other, then froze. Neither of them wanted to look at their bodies, or what was left of them. But Theo bravely ripped off his gloves.

He had flesh underneath, but it was covered with blood.

"What did I do?" Theo cried in anguish. "Did I kill somebody? Did I kill Lisa?"

Roger ignored him for a moment. Instead he turned to Herb and Alexa. "Don't you want to see the real you?" Roger asked Herb. "Wasn't that always your goal?"

Herb nodded but said nothing. He knew he was nothing but dead bone beneath his clothes. He could feel the bareness inside without looking. Nevertheless, he began to pull off his glove. It was Alexa who stopped him—Alexa, whom he'd had a crush on since he was a kid.

"Let me do it for you," she said. "And you can do it for me." She took a breath and looked at the others. "It will be easier that way."

Alexa began to take off his right glove.

He took off hers—

"Herb?" his mother called.

Herb opened his eyes and stared at the ceiling. He was instantly awake. "What?"

"May I come in?"

"Yeah," he said.

His mother opened the door. A glance at her told

7

him she hadn't slept the previous night. There was a deep shadow across her eyes. It was something of a miracle *he* had slept at all, after what had happened.

"There's a Sergeant Fitzsimmons on the phone," she said. "He wants to talk to you."

Herb sat up. "All right. I'll talk to him on my phone."

His mother put her hand to her cheek, where it trembled. "Maybe you shouldn't," she said.

"Why not?"

"Maybe you should talk to a lawyer first."

"Don't worry. It'll be OK."

His mother nodded, and a tear formed in the corner of her eye. She grimaced. "Those poor kids. How did all this happen?"

"I suppose that's what Fitzsimmons wants to find out."

"But he already talked to you last night. Why's he calling again so soon?"

Herb shrugged. "It was late. We hardly went over anything."

"I know it wasn't your fault," she said quickly, wiping the tear from her cheek.

Herb glanced at the black phone sitting on the floor beside his bed. "I probably shouldn't keep him waiting. Could you hang up the other phone for me?"

She nodded. "Be careful, honey" was all she said before leaving.

Herb carefully picked up his receiver. He didn't say anything until he heard his mother put down the phone in her room. Fitzsimmons spoke first.

"You there, Herb?"

"Yeah."

"How are you this morning?"

"OK," Herb said. Big burly Fitzsimmons sounded cheerful enough. Herb had noticed that about him right away, when they had met the day before, when they'd had only one body to explain. Fitzsimmons obviously liked being a cop. He liked doing cop things. Herb figured Fitzsimmons probably watched a lot of cop shows on TV.

"That's good," Fitzsimmons said. "I didn't wake you, did I? Your mom said you might be asleep."

"I was just lying here."

"I always used to sleep in on Saturdays when I was a kid. That was in Boston. Did you know I was from the East?"

Fitzsimmons fit well the average person's stereotype of the ruddy-faced Irish cop. "I guess," Herb said.

"Do you work, Herb?"

"Yeah."

"Part-time job?"

"I go to school and work full-time at a manufacturing warehouse."

"What do you make?"

Herb hesitated. Fitzsimmons wasn't making idle conversation, and Herb knew there was no point in lying. The sergeant could easily check out the facts. "We assemble electronic boards, mostly for VCRs and stuff," Herb said.

"Really? I thought all that stuff was made in Japan."

"The boards are manufactured in Taiwan. We just assemble them."

"Do you know a lot about electronics?" Fitzsimmons asked.

"I know more about photography."

"That's what I hear. They tell me you're a great photographer."

"I guess," Herb said.

Fitzsimmons paused. "What's your schedule look like today?"

"Why?"

"I want you to come down to the station. We've got to talk about what happened."

"I can't come in right now," Herb said.

"Why not?"

"I have someone coming over."

"Who?"

"A friend," he said evasively, then added, "I might be able to come in later."

"I think you should come in now. This is a very serious situation, and I don't think it's over yet. I think you know what I mean."

Herb spoke carefully. "There's no one else to catch."

"Are you sure of that, Herb?"

Herb sat for a moment and listened to his

heartbeat. It sounded awfully loud for a guy who felt so sure of himself. "Why can't we just talk on the phone?" he asked again. Of course Herb knew the answer to that. Fitzsimmons wanted Herb right in front of him when he grilled him. That way it would be easier to tell when he lied.

"How did you sleep last night?" Fitzsimmons asked.

All of a sudden Herb's throat felt tight. "I've slept better."

Fitzsimmons said sympathetically, "It must be tough losing friends like that. It must be even tougher for the families. I talked to a couple of them this morning. Everybody's extremely upset, and they're also terribly confused. I think it could help everybody if we understood how it began. Could you tell me that, Herb?"

Herb closed his eyes and swallowed. His throat was dry. Bone-dry. His dream flashed back to him right then. Roger Corbin riding out of the south like the Grim Reaper on a white horse. Riding toward his friends—skeletons, screaming under a blazing sun.

"Maybe," Herb whispered. "But only on the phone."

"You're a stubborn lad."

"I'm just tired."

Fitzsimmons sighed. "Have it your way then. Where should we begin?"

"With Roger Corbin," Herb blurted out.

"Who's that? Is he related to Theo Corbin? Wait,

isn't he that boy who died six months ago in a car crash?"

"Yeah."

"What does he have to do with any of this?"

"I don't know," Herb said.

"Then why did you bring him up?"

"I had a dream about him last night."

"Herb—"

"He died at that same cliff. Don't you remember?"

Fitzsimmons was silent for a full ten seconds. "But you don't know how this relates to what happened yesterday?"

"No. I'm sorry."

"Tell me what you do know. How did you get involved in all this?"

"I wanted to take pictures of the cheerleaders."

"Yeah."

Herb cleared his throat. "I wanted to take nude pictures of them—if you know what I mean."

"Without their knowing?" Fitzsimmons guessed correctly.

"Yeah."

Fitzsimmons cleared his throat. He might even be smiling, Herb couldn't be sure. All he said was "Tell me the whole story."

CHAPTER ONE

His blood was hot. His thoughts were naughty. Outside, in front of the gymnasium, were Alamo High's cheerleaders, posing prettily for Herb's camera. Inside his head were the same cheerleaders, only in his imagination they were even prettier— they were naked. *Soon* they would be naked. It would be that night that he would set his plan in motion.

His name was Herb Trasker, and if someone had asked him who he was, he would have said "a nobody." His self-esteem was nonexistent. He was eighteen, close to nineteen, and in six weeks he was to graduate from high school. He didn't fool himself into thinking he was handsome, and it was just as well. He stood six-foot-one and weighed in at a hundred and forty pounds. His brown hair was long, unkept, and he couldn't run a comb through it without tearing clumps out. He had never been on a date. He had never even asked a girl out. He was afraid he would be turned down, and it was just as well he realized that. It made Herb a realist.

Yet Herb had one skill that set him apart from most kids. He was an excellent photographer. His mother had given him his first camera when he was twelve—an inexpensive Polaroid that had brought him more pleasure than anything in his life. The camera had come on Christmas, and by New Year's Day he had shot over three hundred pictures—a significant number considering how expensive Polaroid film was and how poor Herb's divorced mother was. He photographed everything—the Christmas tree, the dog, the neighbor's dog, and people—hundreds of people. From the start it was people's faces and bodies that intrigued him the most, and even at the tender age of twelve, he thought women's bodies were the ultimate subjects.

But he wasn't a dirty-minded little snot. He had talent. He had a knack for catching a person's *look*—the particular individual expression or stance that summed up who he or she really was. For example, only two days after that Christmas, he photographed his mother drinking her coffee before leaving for work. His mother hated her job—she was a secretary for a woman-hating general contractor—but she loved her coffee. Herb's picture caught the unhappy lines of her face as she contemplated another week of harassment, just as it showed her hugging her warm cup with a strength that said her hard life was not without its small pleasures. The picture *was* her. She herself said as much when she saw it—just before she ordered him not to take any more pictures of her. That was one thing Herb was to realize at an early age. Catching people on film as they really were was not always flattering or desirable.

At present Herb was photographing the cheer-leaders for the school yearbook. The pictures were late; it was the last week in April and they should have been in at the end of March. A childhood friend of Herb's, Sammie Smith, had shot the original pictures but had messed them up. Herb wasn't sure if she had done it because she was a lousy photographer—which she was—or because Sammie hated the cheerleaders. The rah-rah girls had all come off looking like out-of-focus hookers. The jerks on the yearbook staff had demanded new pictures and ordered Herb onto the scene. Their arrogant tone had annoyed Herb, and he probably would have told them to stuff it if the assignment had not been so choice—and if he had had the guts. If the truth be known, Herb had never told anyone to stuff it in his life.

Yet in a small way, he felt his life was about to come more into focus. It had been Sammie, after hearing he was going to be redoing her shoot, who had given Herb the idea of planting a camera in the girls' showers.

"Fix it up in the corner with an automatic timer on it," Sammie had said. *"I can show you the perfect*

spot. Have it start shooting when they're in the showers. We can save the pictures and distribute them at the graduation party in June. It'll be a nice payback for all the garbage we've had to put up with from those girls the last four years."

Of course Sammie had probably just been kidding, but it got Herb thinking, and Herb hadn't really thought much in the last four years. It was amazing how much energy his brain cells had stored up with the long rest. Once the rush of inspiration washed out the cobwebs, all kinds of possibilities flooded his head. All kinds of bodies. Naked bodies.

"Are you going to make me look pretty?" Alexa Close asked Herb, startling him. She had sneaked up behind him and almost made him drop his camera. She was the last cheerleader out of the locker room. The others were hanging out in the shade of the gymnasium, talking about how far-out they were.

Herb smiled. "That shouldn't be too hard."

Alexa slid around in front of him. She was always sliding from one place to another. She was one graceful girl, and he meant what he had said. All he had to do was remember to take off the lens cap and she'd look pretty. Alexa was the only cheerleader he thought was worth a damn.

"How many pictures are you going to take?" Alexa asked.

"Three rolls should be enough," Herb said. "I'll

shoot some out here on the grass in front of the gym, like you're practicing. Then I thought we could go to different places on campus and take individual shots."

Alexa nodded to his camera. "What kind is that?"

"A Nikon N Twenty-twenty." He added, "It cost a lot of money."

"Did your mom buy it for you?"

"I paid for it myself."

Alexa nodded her approval. "You still working at the electronic plant on Farmer's?"

"Yeah," he replied, pleased she had remembered. Herb had shot Alexa before, when she was putting together a portfolio for modeling agencies in Los Angeles. He'd enjoyed the job—he hadn't wanted to take her money but she had insisted. She was a natural subject, very expressive. She had a long whip of dark brown hair, big red lips, and huge green eyes. She had a way of pouting that made one want to hug and comfort her; then in the next moment she could curl up her lip and look like a vampire preparing for a bite.

Herb thought Alexa would end up as a famous actress one day, if she ever got out of Mannville. Their hometown was a ten-thousand-person hole-in-the-wall, located forty miles east of Sacramento, in the foothills of the Sierras. A few times of the year, especially the spring and fall, it could be beautiful—but it was always boring. It had four fast-food joints, and not one decent restaurant. Its sole movie theater showed flicks that were already available at the video store next door.

Alexa had been impressed with his photos. Yet he still wanted to redo her portfolio, and not just for the pleasure of having her in the center of his lens again. Even though he had caught her in a dozen different moods, he felt he hadn't caught the *real* Alexa yet.

Maybe her clothes got in the way, Herb thought.

He didn't dwell on the idea. It made him feel guilty.

"What hours do you work?" Alexa asked.

"Swing shift," Herb said. "Four to twelve-thirty. Six to two-thirty on Thursdays and Fridays."

"Whew. Tonight's Thursday. I don't see how you make it into school on Fridays. There's no way I could do that."

"I take drugs," Herb said.

Alexa blinked. "Really?"

Herb grinned. "Just kidding." He had smoked dope exactly twice, but stopped when he realized it was called dope for a reason. Herb was a C-minus student and was close to failing history and English. He needed what brains he had. He was anxious to graduate because he had a dream, like Alexa's, of going to L.A. She would become a film star and he would get a job as a photographer. Then one night, years later, they would meet at the premiere of one of her movies, and she would remember him and fall madly in love with him.

Most of Herb's fantasies took place years in the future. It was a safe place. It was safer than the present. Alexa had a boyfriend, Stephen Plead. He had graduated the year before. He was big and stupid and very nasty—he had played football until his junior year when he was kicked off the team for unsportsmanlike behavior. After an unfavorable call, he had picked up a football and heaved it hard into a ref's crotch. Herb had caught the incident on film, but it was a picture he kept in his bedroom closet. He was afraid of Stephen. Just thinking about him made him uncomfortable. But that was a pattern with Herb. Whenever he was around a girl, he would begin to think of all the reasons why she wouldn't want to be around him. Stephen was just one more excuse. Herb lowered his head and fiddled with his camera.

"We should get started," he muttered.

Alexa put a hand on his shoulder. "Are you all right?"

"I'm fine."

Alexa laughed. "I can't figure you out."

Herb was amazed that she'd even bother trying to understand him. He raised his head. "What's there to figure out?" he asked, feeling bold. "What you see is what you get."

She let go of him but held his eye a moment, a grin on her face still. "I don't know about that."

Is she flirting with me?

"Hey," Lisa Barnscull called out. Lisa was head cheerleader and the embodiment of all the clichés of that title. She was blond, bitchy, beautiful, and capable of great cruelty. She was also Alexa's best friend. They were always together. "I'm beginning to sweat," Lisa said. "Let's get started. Quit stroking him, Alexa."

The remark hurt Herb's feelings. But probably Alexa *had* been flirting with him just so he'd take special care photographing her. Alexa glanced over at Lisa and gave her a friendly sneer.

"A little sweat might make you look like you've been working hard," Alexa said.

Lisa gave her a similar sneer. "Hard at what?"

"Hard at what you're good at," Alexa said.

"That could be many things," Lisa said with a nasty smile. Then she paused to regard Herb. Despite her popularity—which was not equivalent to likability—Lisa did not have one particular boyfriend. Her one and only, Roger Corbin, had died in that car crash six months ago. Not that Lisa ever appeared to go into deep mourning. Rumor had her sleeping with half the football team. Herb always felt uncomfortable under her stare.

"What kind of film have you got in that camera?" Lisa asked.

"One hundred," Herb said. "I have a roll of two hundred for the interior shots. Why?"

"I just don't want to have to do this over again," Lisa, who probably knew nothing about film speeds, said.

When Herb had done Alexa's portfolio, he had also done one for Lisa. If Alexa was going to be a model, then Lisa had to be one, too. But maybe the reverse was true. It might have been Lisa's idea to be models. She did appear to be bossier. Herb didn't understand what Alexa saw in her.

Lisa hadn't liked the pictures Herb took of her—at least that had been her excuse for not paying him. She hadn't even compensated him for the cost of the film. He knew he should have demanded the money, but he kept his mouth shut. He knew he had done a good job. Lisa was every bit as pretty as Alexa. With her bright blond hair and big bust, she had a classic California beach girl look. Yet she didn't have Alexa's striking eyes, and Herb knew how that feature, more than any other, prevented one from transferring well to print. The camera simply wasn't kind to Lisa. He had done everything he could with lighting and makeup suggestions to help her out. But he had delivered the prints to the girls at the same time, and Lisa had seen Alexa's first. She felt cheated when she saw her own. That had been three months ago, and since then Lisa never even glanced at him when she passed him in the hall.

"We'll get some good pictures," Herb told Lisa, thinking how much he would enjoy spreading around a nude photo of her at the graduation party. Lisa continued to stare at him, her face now cold.

"Just be sure of it, Herb," she said.

They got to work. Herb took his first roll of group shots with his camera fastened to the top of a tripod. The cheerleader squad was made up of six girls. They were difficult from the word go. With the exception of Alexa, every time Herb got a shot ready, they tried to outdo one another with the size of their smiles. They looked like department store mannequins with toothpicks propping up their cheeks. He told them their natural beauty was more winning than anything they could manufacture, but they acted as if he were an idiot and continued to fake their smiles. Then, when he started on the second roll, Alexa became an unintentional problem. She had a spring allergy and when she started sneezing she couldn't stop. The other girls thought it was funny for a few minutes, then they became impatient. Herb was proud of Alexa. She simply ignored them and went right on sneezing.

Herb took group pictures in front of the gym, inside the gym, and on the football field. In reality he needed only two or three good shots. He had several pictures at home of the girls cheering at a football game. He would add a couple of those to the ones he was taking and the yearbook staff would be happy.

By three o'clock all he had left to do was get a single shot of each girl. He tried being creative. He put one girl cross-legged on a teacher's desk, reading *Romeo and Juliet.* Another he had changing a tire in the auto shop. There was a janitor working; they were able to get in anyplace they wanted. He had another cheerleader climb a tree. The girls finally began to loosen up and stopped acting as if they were doing him a favor by posing for him.

Herb was just about to shoot Alexa's and Lisa's personal portraits when Stephen Plead, Alexa's boyfriend, pulled up in his beat-up red Fiat. From the exhaust, Herb guessed the car was burning at least a quart of oil a day. Stephen didn't stop at the parking lot—he plowed right across the grass to the front of the gymnasium. Insolent as always. Lisa brightened when she saw him, and Alexa hardly reacted at all. That was one thing Herb had noticed when Stephen was around the two girls. Lisa always showed him more attention than Alexa did. He could have been Lisa's boyfriend, for all anyone could tell.

Herb had to grant Stephen one thing. He was handsome, with his Hollywood square jaw and athletic square shoulders. He kept his tan hair cut short like that of a marine, which he acted like. When he spoke, he barked. Yet he mumbled at the same time, which made him sound like a marine who had taken a hit to the head.

"What are you doing?" he growled.

"We're acting out our fantasies in front of Herb," Lisa said.

Stephen scowled at him. "Are you taking their pictures?"

No, I'm using my camera to test their reflexes, Herb thought.

"I'll be done in a few minutes," he muttered out loud instead.

"Don't hurry us," Alexa said to Stephen. "I told you not to come till later."

"Yeah," Lisa said, changing her tone. "Go drive your car around the block a few times, and don't bother us."

Stephen acted slightly annoyed, but didn't defend himself. "I brought the boxes of cookies," he said. "I have them in the trunk. You said you wanted them."

Lisa was suddenly a sweetheart again. She clapped her hands and jumped into the air. She hurried to Herb's side. "I know how you can shoot me and Alexa," she said, excited. "Put us in the home ec room with the cookies. We'll splash ourselves with white flour and put on white caps. We'll go in the yearbook as the Sugar Sisters."

Herb was familiar with the reference. During football season the past fall, Lisa and Alexa had sold home-baked cookies to raise money for the squad. Practically every person in school had bought some because Lisa had a way of making people feel obligated to her. Their venture had been a big success. People had enjoyed the cookies and the squad had been able to pay for whatever it was they needed. It was during this time that Alexa and Lisa had earned the nickname the Sugar Sisters. But then Lisa had continued to sell more cookies, for no charitable purpose except to line Lisa's purse. To top it off, the new cookies were not so good as the first ones. The school administration had finally put a halt to Lisa's activity, angering her.

All this had occurred only a short while after

Roger Corbin, Lisa's boyfriend, had run off the side of a nearby cliff in his car.

"The pictures are supposed to be individual shots like the others I just did," Herb said. "But if you really want—"

"I don't think it's a good idea," Alexa interrupted.

Lisa turned on her. "Why not?"

"I don't want flour all over my clothes," Alexa said.

"Then we'll skip the flour part." Lisa took a step closer to Alexa. "What's the matter? Don't you like the nickname, Alexa?"

Alexa just stared at her. "I like it fine, Lisa."

"The cookies are in the trunk," Stephen said again.

"We know they're in the trunk, idiot," Lisa said.

"Yeah, well, I just thought you should know," Stephen said.

"Are you having another bake sale?" Herb asked.

"Yeah," Lisa snapped, still intent on Alexa.

"What for?" Herb asked.

"We need the money," Lisa said coolly. "What do you say, Alexa?"

Alexa shrugged. "I already said all right."

They went to the home ec room. The janitor let them in, but he warned them to hurry up because he was leaving soon. Stephen followed them like a well-trained mule, toting their boxes of cookies. There seemed to be quite a few of them. Lisa had him spread them over the table and then got aprons and caps for Alexa and herself. Lisa had lied about not using the flour. She immediately tossed a handful over Alexa's head. Alexa no longer seemed to care. She threw a cupful in Lisa's face, and the two girls burst out laughing. Herb took his picture right then. He knew it would be a good one. The Sugar Sisters had been immortalized.

But if Alexa had been sneezing before, now her nose was running continuously. The flour had gotten up her nostrils. Lisa thought it was hysterical, but Stephen was worried about his car.

"All this flour's going to mess up my seats," he said, carrying the cookies back to the car, good mule that he was. Apparently Lisa had decided to take them home and bring them to school the next day. Herb found the whole matter completely illogical. He felt somewhat elated, however. He may have disliked most of the girls on the squad, but they were the *in* people and he had gotten to spend some time with them.

"It's not going to mess up anything," Alexa said. "We'll change before we leave."

"Well, what about your nose?" Stephen asked as if it were a serious problem.

Alexa sneezed. "What about it?"

"My seats are brand-new," Stephen said.

Alexa gave an exasperated groan. "Fine. Herb can give me a ride home. Is that OK, Herb?"

Herb glanced at Stephen, who glared at him in return. It would have been an exciting moment for

Herb, the promise of a drive alone in a car with Alexa. Only he was afraid he might have to pay for it with a rearranged face. The ref Stephen had roughed up had had to spend a week in the hospital.

"If it's all right with everybody else," Herb muttered.

No one complained. Herb assumed it was all right with everybody.

CHAPTER TWO

Alexa changed into white shorts and a blue blouse. Her tan legs were a sight for sore eyes, and they made other parts of Herb ache as well. Herb owned an old Ford Mustang, with cracked upholstery and bald tires. Opening the door for Alexa to climb in, he felt both the thrill of possible romance and the despair of humiliation. Stephen's car might not have been so hot, but next to Herb's jalopy, Stephen's Fiat was a wonder on wheels. Alexa didn't seem to mind. She just asked what year it was.

"A seventy-six," Herb said, getting in himself. "It's got a V-eight engine."

"What can it do on the open road?" Alexa asked, fastening her seat belt.

"The speed limit."

Alexa smiled. "You're not a braggart, are you?"

"I don't know. I know I'm not a mechanic." There was no choice but honesty. As soon as they

hit the road, she would know she was in a hunk of
junk. He added, "The engine's lost half the com-
pression in four of the cylinders. My friend Theo is
going to help me fix it someday. He's great with
cars."

"I know Theo," Alexa said. "He was Roger
Corbin's brother."

"Yeah."

They left the school parking lot. Herb kept
glancing in his rearview mirror, expecting to see
Stephen and Lisa on his tail. But they were nowhere
in sight. He drove with the windows down—his
air-conditioning didn't work. Alexa's long dark
hair brushed his bare arm as it blew in the breeze.

"Do you know where I live?" she asked.

"Yeah."

"I don't want to go home."

"Where do you want to go?" Herb asked.

"Let's get something to eat."

Herb felt instant panic. He got paid that night,
but now he had only ten dollars in his wallet. He
could survive a stop at a fast-food joint, but that
was all. "Where would you like to go?" he asked.

"McDonald's."

"I like McDonald's," he said, relaxing.

Alexa's tastes were similar to his own. She ordered a Big Mac, a large fries, and a strawberry
shake. He had the same, except he made his shake
chocolate. She offered to pay, but he wouldn't hear
of it. They took a booth in the corner. He was

feeling good and she was looking great. She poured a ton of salt on her fries.

"Bad for your heart," he warned.

"I want to die young," she said. "That way I can stay pretty."

"I hear they have excellent preserving techniques these days."

She leaned closer, putting a salt-crusted fry in his mouth. "What I mean is, I like living in the fast lane."

"I usually get honked at when I go into it."

She laughed. "You're hilarious."

Herb tried not to let his pleasure at her compliment show. "Why do you want to live so fast?" he asked.

"Why not? I get bored easy, I guess." She glanced around at the people in the McDonald's—a couple of teenagers and some families, mostly mothers with their squirming kids. "I've been bored since I moved to this city."

"When was that?"

"When I was seven." She made a face. "Don't you remember? We were in second grade together. My first year in Mannville."

The fact was a revelation for Herb. He had no memory of second grade. He didn't have a good memory, period. The earliest he could go back— except for occasional scraps—was fifth grade. Sixth grade was fairly clear. Alexa had been in his sixth-grade class, and even then he'd been entranced by her long shiny ponytails and bright green eyes.

"I can't remember," he said honestly. "I'm terrible that way. That's why I take so many pictures. So I can talk about what's happened."

"Are you serious?"

"I don't know. Are you serious about getting out of this town?"

She nodded. "The day after graduation I'll be on the road heading for L.A."

"Do you have any money saved?"

"None."

"I'd think that would slow you down some."

"Nothing's going to slow me down." She gestured to his camera that he'd brought inside the McDonald's. He never left it alone in the car. "Do you think you got some good shots today?" she asked.

"Yeah."

"When will you develop them?"

"I'll put them in the shop tonight," Herb said.

"I thought you had a darkroom at home. Didn't you develop my portfolio pictures at your house?"

"I can do black and white at home—not color. These are all in color." He smiled. "I think that Sugar Sisters shot is going to come out great."

Alexa wasn't enthusiastic. "Lisa can be so pushy at times."

"Why is she having another cookie sale?"

"For the money. For herself. She wants to beat me to L.A." Alexa paused. "I'm sorry, I shouldn't be putting her down. Nobody likes Lisa, but she's always been a good friend to me. She's been like a sister. And you know how sisters are—they fight about the silliest things. But sometimes we have a serious fight. Did you know we got in a big war when she refused to pay you for the pictures you took?"

Again Herb felt pleasure that his personal existence on the planet had had an effect on Alexa's actions. "I didn't mind," he said.

"But she ripped you off."

"It was only a couple of rolls of film."

"She used your time, your talent."

"If I'd had more talent, it wouldn't have taken me so much time to shoot her." He shrugged. "It was good practice for me."

Alexa was watching him. "Practice for what?"

"Being a photographer." He didn't know why she was suddenly studying him. Surely she had no idea of his plan to plant his camera in the girls' showers. He wasn't even sure if he was still going to go through with it. The more he talked to Alexa, the less he liked the idea of taking advantage of her. He lowered his head, adding, "I'm going to try to get a job with an L.A. paper after graduation."

"You're going to follow me there," she said.

"Not unless I get there before you."

She spoke abruptly. "You wonder what I'm doing with Stephen."

She had caught him off guard with her changing subjects so quickly. He had never heard Alexa so blunt. "Not at all. He seems like a nice guy."

"He's an idiot."

"Then why are you going out with him?"

"Idiots can be fun." Her smile returned. "And Lisa likes him."

"Huh?"

Alexa wasn't given a chance to elaborate further because Sammie Smith appeared out of nowhere just then. Herb silently cursed her and her lousy timing. He'd known Sammie forever. She had hung out with Theo and him since they were kids exploring the hills surrounding Mannville. Back then she had been a tomboy, and she'd grown up not entirely feminine. First there were her clothes. She dressed like an ex-convict, a male ex-convict. She was fond of wearing sweatshirts even on ninety-degree days. That day she had on an extra-large, long-sleeved wool shirt with a stencil of Fred Flintstone on the front.

Sammie was also overweight. She didn't have a body, her body had her. Somewhere inside, hidden beneath the rolls of fat, was the real Sammie. She could have been an attractive girl—Herb knew because he'd seen her baby pictures. He'd seen her *when* she was a baby, although that time period naturally lay outside the domain of his higher brain centers. Her hair was light brown, healthy enough, but cut like a dish towel that had fallen into a garbage disposal. She had bangs that had grown into tangled strings that spent most of their time collecting sweat. She never wore make-up. She said she was allergic to it, but Herb thought she simply didn't know how to put it on.

Or if she did put it on, it would show that she cared, and above all else, Sammie Smith didn't want anyone to know she cared what anybody thought about her.

But she wasn't Herb's friend without reason. She was loyal. If he was ever in a bind, with money or his car or anything, Sammie was there in a flash to help out. She was also very funny, especially when she was together with Theo. Their humor was often biting, and their victims were always the more popular kids on campus. The jokes they told usually did possess strong character insights, though. They'd had a lot of fun when the Sugar Sisters were peddling their cookies earlier in the year. Sammie had said from the beginning that Lisa was stealing most of the money. Yet Sammie never said these things within hearing distance of Lisa. If anything, Sammie always treated Lisa with too much respect.

Herb didn't know how Sammie felt about Alexa.

"How are you doing?" Sammie asked, ambling up to the table, a large Coke in her hand. Sammie could eat two Big Macs in a sitting, and have room for a third, plus dessert.

"Great," Herb said. He gestured with his hand to Alexa. "You know Alexa, don't you?"

Sammie hardly looked at her. "Yeah."

"How have you been, Samantha?" Alexa asked sweetly.

Sammie shuffled uneasily. "Not bad. What are you guys doing here?"

You mean, what am I doing here with a girl as beautiful as Alexa? I'm wondering that myself.

"Eating health food," Alexa said, sipping her shake.

"We just did the shoot on the cheerleaders," Herb said.

Sammie grinned nervously. "Oh, yeah, the one I messed up."

"I think Herb caught us in our full glory today," Alexa said, licking the shake from her lush lips. Sammie gave Herb a quick glance, but Herb wisely chose not to react. Alexa's reference had been coincidental, he thought, and never mind that the slang "full glory" referred to people who were stark naked. Still, the comment gave him further doubts about his plan, or rather, Sammie's plan. He reminded himself that it had been her idea.

"I tried my best," Herb said.

"I've already finished eating," Sammie said out of nowhere, obviously nervous.

"That's too bad," Alexa said. "You could have joined us."

"Yeah, that's horrible," Herb said. "I mean, it's a shame. Where're you going now?"

He wasn't being very subtle. He couldn't imagine anything worse than Sammie joining them. She was his friend, but he saw her every day. He talked to Alexa every two years. Sammie appeared to take the hint—at least that was how it seemed at first.

"I have to get home," she said. "I've got work to do."

"Goodbye," Alexa said smoothly.

"Catch you later," Herb said, half rising from his seat.

Sammie nodded and slumped away. Herb thought they had done her a favor by chasing her off because she had been distinctly uncomfortable in Alexa's presence.

Yet Sammie was back a minute later, saying she needed a ride. Her car wouldn't start.

"What's wrong with it?" Herb asked.

"I don't know," Sammie said.

"What sound does it make when you turn the key?" Herb asked.

"It doesn't do anything," Sammie said.

"Sounds like the battery then," Herb said. "Maybe all you need is a jump. I have my cables with me."

"No," Sammie said. "I don't want to mess with it. I want Theo to look at it. He can always get it running. Just give me a ride home." She added quickly, "If you would, please."

"Sure," Herb said.

"Can we finish eating first?" Alexa asked.

"I don't care," Sammie said. She sat down beside Herb and stared off into the distance. "Take your time."

From that point on the conversation ground down. If anything, Sammie's uneasiness in Alexa's presence worsened. Sammie seemed to sweat just hearing her voice. Yet Herb suspected Sammie was clinging to them on purpose, but he couldn't imagine why. Alexa didn't seem to notice, or if she did, she didn't care.

They finished their food and went outside. Sammie wouldn't even let Herb have a peek at her car, which deepened his suspicions. To make matters worse, Sammie began to drop hints that she had to talk to him. She obviously wanted him to drop Alexa off first, and it did make sense in a way. Alexa lived far from him, and Sammie was only around the block. Yet Herb's resentment of the intrusion grew stronger. Alexa appeared in no hurry to get home. If Sammie hadn't appeared, they probably could have talked longer.

Alexa lived in "the heights." All of Mannville was in the hills, but naturally some of the houses were higher up. To reach Alexa's home, Herb had to climb a narrow asphalt road a mile and half out of the town. He remembered that Lisa also lived in the heights, but he couldn't recall where.

Alexa was friendly as she got out of his car at the end of her driveway. "I really appreciate the ride and the food," she said. "I'll have to repay the favor soon."

"It was no problem," Herb said. "I'll show you the pictures as soon as I get them back. Maybe you can pick out the ones you want in the yearbook."

Alexa laughed. "No, I'll leave the selection to you. It was nice to see you again, Samantha."

"Yeah, it was fun," Sammie said flatly, climbing into the front seat.

Alexa began to walk toward her front door, looking awfully sexy in her shorts. "Goodbye, Herb," she said over her shoulder. "Take care."

"You, too," he said.

When they were heading back down the hill, Sammie spoke up. "What was that all about?" she asked.

"What?"

"Why were you driving Alexa Close home? Why were you feeding Alexa Close?"

"She needed a ride and she was hungry."

Sammie pulled out a cigarette. "I just find that weird. She doesn't even like you."

Herb swallowed. "You don't know her."

Sammie had lost her timidity. "Oh, get off it. She's a rah-rah. She doesn't have friends. She collects objects to use and compensate for her lack of intelligence and personality."

Herb shrugged. "I don't think she's so bad."

Sammie stared incredulously at him. "Do you like this girl or something?"

"I hardly know her."

"I can't believe you, Herb."

"Well, what's wrong with her?"

Sammie sat back. "Nothing. She's perfect. She's a goddamn piece of art." Sammie flicked ash out the window. "Have you thought any more about how you're going to do it?"

"Do what?"

"Take the pictures."

"I don't know if I'm going to."

"Why not?" Sammie sneered. "Do it tomorrow and you'll get one of your girlfriend."

Herb tried to concentrate on the road. "What's so special about tomorrow? Why can't I do it any day?"

Sammie was impatient. "I told you, Fridays the cheerleaders go through their entire routine. It's a full workout. It's one of the few days you can be sure they're going to take showers afterward." Sammie paused. "Set your equipment tonight and you can have the pictures tomorrow."

"The equipment isn't that easy. I don't have a time-lapse attachment."

"I know that," Sammie said. "But I thought you said you could build something that would work just as well."

"Why are you so anxious to have these pictures taken?"

"Why are you so afraid? When I talked to you about it a few days ago, you were bouncing off the walls."

"That's not true," Herb said.

"You were excited."

"I have to think about it some more. Don't bother me about it right now. Do you want me to go check on your car now that Alexa's gone?"

Sammie continued to regard him critically. "You don't think there's anything wrong with it, do you?"

"What are you talking about? You said it wouldn't start. If it won't start, it won't start."

Sammie threw her cigarette out the window. "You can drive over and try to start it if you want, I don't care."

Herb didn't bother trying. He just took Sammie straight home. He didn't understand why she was in such a bad mood, and she didn't say one funny thing the whole way.

Herb didn't get home until five-thirty, and he had to be at work in half an hour. His mother was already home. He bumped into her in the kitchen, where she was making him dinner—broiled chicken and wild rice. She was great that way, and at the same time terrible. She would make him dinner when she knew he had no time to eat or when he wasn't hungry, just because it was what a good mother did. He would always find the time and room to eat at least some of it, because he was a good son.

She kissed him hello, which always embarrassed him. He had stopped feeling comfortable with her gestures of affection in seventh grade, when he'd started thinking about sex all the time.

His mother was a handsome woman, much more attractive than he was. He had inherited too many of his father's genes. Besides being a two-timing scoundrel, his father had been a nondescript individual. He had split eight years ago, and Herb only thought about him at Christmas when the old man sent him a twenty-dollar bill. Yeah, twenty dollars without fail, and never even a note to apologize for the effects of inflation on the annual gift.

His father had been a fool to leave his mother. She was forty-three, and had a figure every bit as good as the cheerleaders he had photographed that afternoon. There wasn't a hint of gray in her dark hair, and if it was because she regularly dyed it, it didn't matter. Her secretarial job often tired her out and made her grumpy. She dreamed of owning her own business and being her own boss. But neither her fatigue nor her unfulfilled dreams obscured her intrinsic honesty and kindness. She took good care of him. He tried to take care of her. He gave her half his paycheck. When they got right down to it, they had only each other.

"You're late," she said after planting her kiss.

"I had to photograph the cheerleaders," he answered, setting his camera down on the kitchen table and taking the rolls of film out of his pocket.

"Hard work. Did any of them flash you?"

"Yeah, two of them did. The click of the shutter really gets them excited."

"Are you hungry? Do you have time to eat?"

He wondered how he could shove anything more down as she took the chicken from the oven and reached for the pot of rice. "Sure," he said. "But let me jump in the shower for a few minutes first." Maybe some of his shake and hamburger would settle by then.

Their home was snuggled in at the end of a cul-de-sac, at the base of a small cluster of brush-covered hills. Their backyard opened into wide open territory, and the nearest house was over a hundred yards away. The location of the house was wonderful, but unfortunately, the house itself possessed only two small bedrooms and one tired bathroom. The latter was desperately in need of fresh wallpaper. The old stuff had begun to *fuse* into the paint underneath. He decided he would surprise her with new paper.

Herb was scrubbing himself with a bar of soap, wondering what kind of paper his mother would like, when the gun went off.

"God!" he shouted, jumping straight up and almost slipping and falling. It took him a few seconds to realize that they weren't under attack, that it was just Theo Corbin taking target practice in their backyard. Herb hated sudden shocks. He had a frail constitution. Even though he'd figured out what was going on, his heart continued to pound uncontrollably. He stepped out of the shower and poked his head out the window. Theo had his rifle up and was aiming at one of three Coke cans he had set up on a boulder at the far edge of their property.

"You wouldn't want to knock first, would you?" Herb called.

Theo looked around, trying to find Herb. When he finally spotted him, he answered, "I told your mom I was going to shoot."

"That did me a lot of good." He and Theo worked in the same place, the same hours. They often rode to the factory together. But Herb hadn't planned on taking Theo with him tonight. He hadn't planned on telling Theo about the pictures he hoped to take, at least not until he had them in hand. Theo's ethics varied from week to week, but on the whole they were more conservative than Herb's. Theo had become particularly sensitive about what was right and wrong since his brother died. On the other hand, there was nothing Theo liked better than a good-looking girl.

Theo was short and thin and had a tiny head. His head was so small it was a wonder God had found room to stuff brains inside. But Herb was smart enough to recognize that Theo had the better share of gray matter. Theo wasted his sharp mind, however, and his grades were as dismal as Herb's. They had gotten worse since his brother died. There was even some question about whether Theo would graduate in June. He acted his usual crazy self on the outside, but under his jokes and witty remarks, it was clear to Herb that he was putting on an act. Theo was lost without Roger. He drank too much beer. He spent too much time shooting his gun at the Coke cans he pretended were Lisa Barnscull's face.

There wasn't a single shred of evidence to link Roger's fatal car accident with Lisa. She hadn't been with him at the time. According to Sammie, an objective source if there was one, Lisa hadn't even been in the area. When Roger had nose-dived off the cliff on the way to Mannville's heights, he was completely alone, except for the two grams of cocaine bubbling through his bloodstream. And that's what got to Theo. He swore his brother never used drugs, that Lisa was the coke freak, that she must have forced Roger to take it. Herb tried to reason with him. No one, he said, much less a thin blond girl, could squeeze that much coke into a well-built nineteen-year-old guy. Roger had gone off the cliff because he was loaded, pure and simple. It was a terrible accident.

Yet Theo still didn't believe it, and one of these days, he said, he was going to get Lisa. Herb didn't take the threat too seriously. He had gone hunting with Theo a couple of times. Theo was a hell of a shot. He could hit a can of soda at five hundred feet. But he wasn't a hunter. He'd line up a jackrabbit in his sights and hit the blade of grass in the rabbit's mouth instead. Theo couldn't even talk tough, not really. He said he'd get Lisa and then he'd flush red with shame.

Theo had missed the Coke can on his first shot, the one that had sent Herb's heart pounding. As Herb watched him take aim again, he wondered if Theo's using Coke cans for targets had anything to do with the drug that had been found in his brother's body. Theo pulled the trigger and the can on the far right exploded.

"Did I make you pee in your pants?" Theo asked.

"I don't wear pants in the shower," Herb said.

Theo checked his watch. "You should get dressed. We're going to be late."

"Why don't you just go ahead without me," Herb

said. "My mom's made me dinner and I have film I want to drop off before I go in."

Theo shrugged and took aim at another can. "If you're going to be late I might as well be late. Besides, I'm hungry. Maybe your mom will feed me, too."

Herb preferred to postpone decisions, and he felt he was being forced to make up his mind now. He couldn't take both Theo and the equipment he needed to shoot the girls in the showers home from work. In a way, Theo's forcing him to decide should have put his mind at ease. The decision was being made for him. But despite all his guilt about taking advantage of Alexa, he really wanted the pictures. He had drooled over dozens of *Playboy* magazines in his days, but he had never seen a girl he personally knew naked. He could imagine the thrill of it, but he wanted the reality. If he did happen to catch Alexa on film, he told himself he could always destroy those frames. He wouldn't even have to look at them. Certainly, he wouldn't let Sammie get her hands on them.

"I'm going to be real late to work, maybe forty minutes," Herb said. "I really think you should go on without me."

Theo blew away the middle can. The brown foam poured over the rock like bad booze. "I walked over here," Theo said, lowering his rifle. "If I walk back to get my car, I'll be a lot later than forty minutes."

"You walked over here carrying your rifle?"

"No, I left it here a few days ago. Don't you remember?"

"No," Herb said. "But it doesn't matter—I'll give you a ride to your house." Then Herb would have to come back home again and get his camera and stuff. Theo knew Herb would never—under normal circumstances—bring his camera to work.

Theo smiled and took a step toward him. "You really don't want me to come with you, do you? Where are you going after work?"

"Nowhere."

"I heard you were at McDonald's with Alexa Close," Theo said.

"Who told you that? Sammie?"

"No. But news spreads fast in this town. How did you manage to get Alexa to eat with you?"

"I didn't *get* her to eat with me. She wanted something to eat so we stopped. It's no big deal."

Theo set his gun down against the wall of the house. Because of her close friendship with Lisa, Alexa wasn't a favorite of Theo's. Yet he seemed to warm to the girl as they spoke.

"Did you have fun?" Theo asked.

"The food was good."

Theo sneered. "Did she have fun?"

"I don't know. Why don't you ask her?"

"Did Stephen know you were with her?"

"Yeah. He was there when she asked if I would give her a ride home."

"Why didn't she go home with him?" Theo asked.

"Because he was worried about his seats."

"Herb, this is your best friend you're talking to. Why don't you just tell me the story straight?"

"I am. There's nothing to tell. She needed a ride home and I gave her one. She was hungry and I bought her food. We didn't go out or anything."

"Did you ask her out when you were finished doing all these other things for her?"

"No."

"Why not? You've been talking about her for years."

"Because she has a boyfriend," Herb said. "And he's bigger than me. Now shut up and let me finish my shower. If you're hungry, go inside. The chicken's already sitting on the table. Tell my mom I'll be there in a few minutes. Put your gun away. Put it in the garage."

Herb finished his shower and dressed quickly. Once in the kitchen he only managed a couple of chicken wings and a handful of rice. Theo wouldn't let up on him even at the table. He told Herb's mom that Herb had already eaten that afternoon with a beautiful girl. Herb's mom was interested in hearing the details, but Herb was evasive.

Herb did drive Theo home, and by this time Theo was convinced Herb was going somewhere after work. Herb was wondering if there was any chance he would be able to place his camera that night. Theo was a good friend, but he could be a pain in the ass at the exact right time.

Herb dashed back in his house a few minutes

later and told his mom he had forgotten the film he was taking to be developed. He slipped his camera into a black carrying case and stuffed his camera cable in his pocket. The camera cable was used for taking pictures from a distance of a few feet. Well, he thought, if he did get everything set up and didn't change his mind, he would be more than a few miles away from his equipment when he took his most exciting pictures.

CHAPTER THREE

In the End

"Can I stop you for a minute?" Sergeant Fitz-simmons asked.

"Sure," Herb said.

"Why were you doing all this?"

"All what?"

"Why were you going to all this trouble to take these pictures? I mean, I can understand why any teenage boy would want photos of a bunch of naked cheerleaders. Hell, I'd probably look at them myself. But the way you talk about it, you seemed to swing from being all excited about the idea to feeling guilty about it."

"Is that unusual?"

"In a way. Let me ask you something. How much pressure did Sammie put on you to take the pictures?"

"Some, not much."

"But she wanted you to take them that Friday afternoon? Any other day wouldn't do?"

"Yeah."

"Did that make you suspicious?" Fitzsimmons asked.

"Not then. But later, yeah. It made me wonder."

"I'm probably getting ahead of myself. I should let you finish your story. But I'm curious how you were able to take the pictures. You said you didn't have time-lapse equipment?"

"No. That stuff's expensive," Herb said. "But I was able to put together equipment that worked just as well." He paused. "Do you need to hear all the details?"

"Yeah."

"Is this off the record?"

Fitzsimmons thought a moment. "I can't promise you that."

"Then maybe I'm getting myself in too deep. Maybe I should talk to a lawyer first."

"Herb, were you directly or indirectly responsible for any of the deaths that occurred yesterday?"

"I might have been indirectly responsible."

"I don't think so," Fitzsimmons said.

"How do you know? I haven't even begun to tell you what happened."

"Let's just say I know. Herb, you can trust me with this information."

"But what's the law against Peeping Toms?"

"I'd have to look it up."

"Well, say I did take these pictures. Does that mean I've broken the law?"

"Do you care if you have, after all that's happened?"

The tightness in Herb's throat returned. He remembered stepping in the puddle of blood the night before and knowing that the puddle was too vast to ever drip back into the body crumpled beside it. He remembered the smell of the blood, mixed with the dirt on the cliff top, and how different it smelled from the burnt flesh of a few hours earlier.

"I guess not," Herb said. He had to take a breath. "I rigged my camera up to a VCR."

"Come again?" Fitzsimmons said.

"I needed a way to have my camera snap several pictures during a certain time frame. I thought of all these complex electrical ways of triggering the camera, but that was the trouble with them—they were all too complex. I told you at work we put together VCRs. Well, just about any VCR can be programmed to record a half dozen TV shows. What I did was solder the bare wires of my camera cable to—"

"What's a camera cable?" Fitzsimmons asked.

"It's a cable that allows you to stand several feet away from the camera and take a picture."

"Like if you want to be in the picture yourself?"

"It can be used to do that. But usually if you want to be in the picture you just have a twenty-second delay on the snap."

"Does your camera have such a delay feature built into it?"

"Yeah."

"Couldn't you have just lengthened the delay so that it went off hours later instead of seconds?"

"I don't think so. Even if I could have, it would have been no good for what I needed. I needed to shoot several pictures over a period of time because I couldn't tell exactly when the cheerleaders would get in the shower. The VCRs we assemble at work can be programmed to record eight different shows. I soldered the wires of my camera cable onto the heads of a VCR. Every time it came to one of the program times, the VCR moved its heads and pressed the cable wires together, and a picture was taken."

"So you set it to take eight pictures?"

"That's the maximum the VCR would allow. I set it to take a picture every four minutes, starting at four o'clock even. The last picture was snapped at four twenty-eight."

"You mean four thirty-two?"

"No. Four twenty-eight. You can figure it out on a piece of paper."

"I see. Who told you the cheerleaders would be in the showers at four o'clock?"

Herb hesitated. "Sammie did."

Fitzsimmons sounded as if he were taking notes. "When did you set all this equipment up in the showers?"

"Late Thursday night. Early Friday morning."

"Can you be more exact?" Fitzsimmons asked.

"Three o'clock Friday morning."

"Did anyone help you?"

"No," Herb said.

"Did anyone see you place the equipment?"

"I don't know. I don't think so."

"How did you hide all this equipment so that no one could see it? And how did you get into the girls' showers?"

"Let me tell you, it wasn't easy," Herb said.

CHAPTER FOUR

Work was dull. Herb found it difficult to concentrate. Not that he needed much of his mind to do his job. His major function as a minimum wage employee was to solder chips on electronic boards. Since he had soldered the same chips on the same boards for over a year, he could do it in his sleep. Sometimes he *did* do it in his sleep. He dreamed about the chips and the boards and the smell of the solder. He had read somewhere that solder fumes were highly carcinogenic. He could honestly say he had no plans to make the job his life's work.

But there were pluses to the job. Because he worked the swing shift, he never saw the main boss, who left at five o'clock on Thursdays and Fridays. The guy who oversaw Herb's shift was only three years older than Herb. He was a totally laid-back dude, who drank a six-pack every night. Herb hadn't minded that until the guy started bringing in beer for Theo. Theo couldn't solder after he'd had a few cans, so Herb had to do Theo's job on top of his own so Theo wouldn't get fired. Theo's family needed his measly paycheck. Theo's dad worked in construction, and Mannville put up a new building every six months, and it was usually the size of an outhouse.

Another advantage to the swing shift was the music. They got to listen to the radio—loud. Herb normally liked to have rock on. But that Thursday night the music was just giving him a headache. He was trying to plan the details of his Peeping Tom escapade, and solder fumes were burning the cartilage in his nose, and the Rolling Stones were screaming. It had always been hard for him to do two things at once.

He wasn't worrying, however, about wiring his camera cable to the heads of the VCR—he knew he could do that in a few minutes. He was most concerned about sneaking the VCR out of the warehouse, especially with Theo watching him. Then there was the problem of getting inside the girls' shower room. Sammie had said the tree at the back of the showers was as good as a ladder to the upper windows, but even a ladder could be hard to climb with pounds of awkward equipment. Herb had a feeling it was going to be a long night.

Finally there was his continuing indecision. He would make up his mind he was going to do it—he *had* made up his mind—but then he'd remember how kind Alexa had been to him and how she'd feel if she knew what he was doing. Yet, paradoxically, the thought of Alexa would just drive him to do it more. Of course, it was no paradox at all. Alexa had been kind to him, but he knew he was never going to get closer to her than he had already. The next best thing would be the pictures, he thought.

"Spacing out?" Theo asked from across the cluttered workbench.

"Look who's talking," Herb said. It was close to eleven o'clock. "How many beers have you had?"

"I can't remember." Theo took a sip from the can sitting beside his electronic board and grinned. "I suppose that means I've had one too many." He set the can back down. "I'm really disappointed in you, Herb."

"I'm not going to ask why," Herb replied, reaching for a fresh board. When he was not soldering on the chips, he tested the boards to see if the other employees in the warehouse had soldered them on correctly. Six other guys, all close to his age, worked the swing shift. The testing machine required only that a board be slipped inside. If the light shone green, it was OK. If not, the light blinked red. A chimpanzee could have been in charge of quality control.

"At least you could tell me *something* about your date with Alexa," Theo went on. He insisted upon calling it a "date" and there was no point in correcting him. "What did she eat?"

"A hamburger, french fries, and a strawberry shake."

"Did you pay for it?"

"Yeah," Herb said.

"Well, then she owes you something."

"Like what?"

"Sex," Theo said.

"Get off it."

Theo sat back from his work, thinking. "Herb, can I ask you a personal question?"

"No, I didn't have sex with Alexa at McDonald's."

"Do you think we're ever going to have girlfriends?"

Herb glanced around to make sure no one else was listening. The high volume of the music took care of that possibility. Herb could see Theo was serious. "What are you talking about?" he asked. "You've already had a girlfriend. What about Marjorie Bennett?"

Theo waved his hand. "She was just someone I ate fast food with. Besides, she was a tramp. I mean real girlfriends, someone we could marry someday. Do you think we'll ever have those?"

Herb did think about it a minute. "We'll probably get married someday—just about everyone does. But it'll probably be to someone other than the person we really want to marry."

Theo nodded. "I think you're right. It's depressing, huh?"

"Yeah."

"Would you marry Alexa right now if you could?"

"I'm too young, and too broke."

"Say you were a few years older and had a good job. Knowing her as well as you do now, would you want to marry her?"

"That's the stupidest question I ever heard."

"I'm serious. Would you want her for keeps?"

Herb smiled faintly. "I wouldn't mind looking at her for a few years."

Theo nodded again. "But we're just losers, aren't we? We'll never have a good job. We'll never look any better than we do now." Theo sighed. "That was one thing my brother had going for him. He was so goddamn handsome the girls couldn't keep their eyes off him." He lowered his head, poking at the electronic board in front of him with his soldering gun. "That goddamn Lisa."

"Lisa wasn't there. She was at the movies in Parvo. Sammie saw her there. Sammie wouldn't lie about it."

Theo shook his head. "I don't care if she was in the area or not. Roger was a different person before he met Lisa. He wasn't all stressed out. He always watched where he was going." Theo set down his board and closed his eyes, his right hand tightening into a fist. He didn't pound the table, however. He just put the fist up to the side of his head, as if he wished he could pound something out of his mind. "I wish I knew where he'd been that day."

58

"Let it go, Theo."

Theo opened his eyes. "Do you think Alexa would know?"

"Huh? How would Alexa know?"

"She's Lisa's best friend." He was getting excited. "Could you ask her for me?"

"No. I can't ask her something like that. Anyway, didn't Sammie say Alexa was with Lisa at the movies in Parvo? Yeah, I think she did. Why don't you ask Sammie about it first."

Theo showed impatience. "I know Alexa was with Lisa. That's what the whole goddamn school knows. But that's not what I'm asking. Alexa still may have known where Roger was that day. Lisa probably knew. She might have told Alexa. Why can't you ask her for me?"

"All right. I'll ask her if it means that much to you."

"Can you do it right away? Like tomorrow?" Theo asked.

"What's the hurry?"

"Just do it, all right! Do I ever ask you for favors?"

"I'll do it," Herb said. It was true Theo never asked for anything. But, boy, was everybody in a hurry. Do it tonight, Herb. Do it tomorrow. One would think there was an important deadline coming up.

At two o'clock, half an hour before quitting time, Herb grabbed a bunch of electronic boards and walked over to the testing machine, which was located in a separate room near the back door. By that time Theo had finished a few more beers and lost interest in the universe as a whole. Herb was hardly in the testing room a minute when he slipped out to his car and got his camera and camera cable. The previous day he had placed an expensive—meaning, highly programmable—VCR in the testing room. At the present he had his own personal soldering gun in his pocket, plus a coil of solder. The camera-VCR fusion took more than the few minutes he had anticipated, but he had the equipment together before the rest of the guys began to punch out. In fact, he had no trouble sneaking out to his car and hiding the whole lot in his trunk. It was at this point that he began to feel committed. He was, after all, stealing a four-hundred-dollar piece of electronic equipment for the next twenty-four hours. He had never stolen anything in his life before.

Theo revived somewhat as they walked in the cool air toward their cars. He wanted to go for breakfast at the Denny's on Mannville's main strip. They often did this after their late Thursday shift. Sometimes they'd sit in Denny's and drink coffee until the sun came up.

But Herb wasn't in the mood for breakfast. He had trees to climb. "I'm tired," he said, pulling his keys from his pants pocket. He had on his favorite pair of blue jeans, the ones he washed every six months, whether they needed it or not. "I don't have any money. I think I'll just go home and crash."

"I've got a few dollars," Theo said, following him to his car. "Come on, Alexa's got to be asleep by now."

"Would you drop that crap." Herb opened his car door and turned to take a look at his friend. He felt guilty making Theo drive himself home when he'd had so much to drink. Indeed, one of the reasons they had started driving to work together was so Theo would get home in one piece. "You look like you're ready to fall over," he added. "You should rest. Get in your car, I'll follow you home."

But Theo took a step back. "No, I want some bacon and eggs. I'll go by myself." He turned away.

"Theo," Herb called.

"Say hello to Alexa for me," Theo called back.

Herb watched Theo leave the parking lot. He didn't follow him. He had been telling the truth when he said he was tired. He wanted to get to the school, set his equipment up, and go to bed as soon as possible. As he started his car he hoped he wouldn't end up in jail before he could get home.

There wasn't a car in the school parking lot. Herb noticed that the wide gate leading to the gymnasium and the showers was still open. Following Stephen's example from that afternoon, he simply drove through the gate and up onto the grass. He parked less than fifty feet from the girls' showers. Mannville didn't have its own police station, and the cop who patrolled the area probably never stopped to walk the school's empty halls in the dead of night. To be extra careful, though, Herb jogged back to the gate after he parked and closed the gate over, presenting the illusion that it was locked. Now he could work undisturbed.

Herb kept a flashlight in his glove compartment, along with a pair of pliers, a couple of screwdrivers, and various other things. It was a dark and moonless night, and the lights around the showers had burned out two years earlier. Unfortunately, the batteries in his flashlight had been almost squeezed of their last drops of juice. What the feeble light did show was that the tree Sammie had told him about—and which he should have studied in greater detail earlier—did indeed lead directly up to the upper windows of the shower room. But the tree had not been designed to be climbed with only one free hand. Herb decided he had to climb up first, get the window open, and then come back for his equipment.

Herb did take his screwdrivers and flashlight with him as he made his way up the first time. He was not exceptionally coordinated—plus he was afraid of heights. When he was ten feet above the ground, he paused to look down and instantly became dizzy. He had to grab a branch to steady himself. He often fantasized about being a James Bond–type hero, but this he did only while sitting down. He silently began to curse Sammie for giving him the crazy idea of photographing the cheerleaders in the buff.

The casement windows in the girls' shower room were similar to the ones in the boys', and those he *had* studied earlier. The windows only tilted in so far, at best forty-five degrees. He figured if he was to climb inside, he would have to remove at least one of the windows.

It was a pity he didn't stick with his initial evaluation. When he reached the limb of the tree that peeked inside the windows, and found that one of the windows was all the way open, he couldn't resist trying to squeeze inside. Of course he immediately got stuck. It was ridiculous. It was embarrassing. Worse, it hurt. As he tried squirming back out, the rusty edge of the window dug under the belly of his T-shirt and scratched him.

"God," he muttered, as his feet began to slip on the tree branch somewhere beneath him. The age of the window hinges eventually came to his rescue, if it could be called a rescue. The right hinges snapped, and the left ones followed only a fraction of a second behind them. The window dropped beneath him, and fell away, exploding on the floor below. Herb quickly grasped the window frame so he wouldn't topple forward and join the glass shards on the floor below. He was *very* happy that he was going to get in and out without leaving any clues. Ha!

Now I'll have to find a broom to sweep up that

mess. God, someone might notice the missing window right away, and get a ladder, and find my equipment.

He had to look on the bright side. At least now he had a clear opening into the showers. He climbed back down the tree to fetch the VCR and camera. Now he began to feel uneasy—his camera was more important to him than his left leg. If he dropped it, he'd die. He stared up at the dark tree for several minutes before deciding what to do next.

He had a piece of rope in his trunk. He figured he could tie the VCR to his back and snuggle his camera inside his shirt. And that's what he did, except the VCR began to untie itself just as he reached the open window. He was lucky he was able to stop and catch it.

There was a two-foot ledge on the other side of the window, as there was in the boys' showers as well. Without that ledge, the whole plan would have been hopeless. It was a pity, he thought, that the window he had knocked free hadn't landed on the ledge. The ledge led directly into an even larger corner ledge, off to the left, which was where Sammie had told him to hide his equipment. Hugging the VCR to his side, Herb tentatively swung a leg over the edge of the window and ducked his head through the opening. The ledge was firm beneath his foot. He pulled his other leg through the window and stood up cautiously.

He was inside.

Herb pulled out his flashlight. It might have been better if he'd left it in his pocket turned off. Even the weak batteries were strong enough to give him a clear picture of how far he'd fall if he took a false step—fifteen feet, if not more. He shuffled carefully toward the corner, his feet pointed straight out in front of him. He didn't have far to go—twelve feet at most. A few seconds later he was crouched in the wide space of the corner and was able to set his stuff down.

The corner ledge was exceptionally wide because it had once been used as a platform for an air compressor. Herb didn't know why the architect had placed the machine so high up, but he could see why safety officials had demanded that it be removed to the floor behind the showers. Herb was directly above where the girls washed. If the platform had given out at an inopportune time, the equipment could have crushed somebody. There were still two perpendicular metal plates in the corner that had helped to hold the compressor in place. It was behind one of these that Herb set the VCR.

Another advantage of the corner ledge was that there was an electrical outlet available near it. Herb had hoped that he could use the outlet to power the VCR. Regrettably, after plugging the VCR in and having nothing happen, Herb realized he was dealing with a dead outlet. It was a setback to his plan, but not a catastrophe. He had anticipated that the outlet might not work, so he had brought along a fifty-foot extension cord. It was outside in the trunk of his car. There was another socket relatively close that Sammie had told him would work. It was located in the girls' equipment locker, which stood adjacent to the actual showers, on his side of the room. The equipment locker was a fifteen-foot-square metal cage. It was called a locker but it was never locked. Sammie had told him that he could feed an extension cord into the back of the cage and plug it in there. The danger was, of course, that someone would see the cord and follow it up to his equipment. But he had the time of the year going for him. It wasn't football season, or even basketball season, when girls were going in and out of the cage for all kinds of stuff. For just a day, though, the cord should remain undisturbed. That was Sammie's opinion.

Herb went back outside and down the tree to get the extension cord. It was while he was climbing back in through the window that he got the idea that there was no reason why he should work in the dark. He would have to turn on the lights anyway to focus his camera on the spot he wanted to shoot. Rather than heading immediately back to the corner, he carefully shuffled in the other direction, until he came to the tiled wall that separated the showers from the lockers. It was at this point his flashlight failed completely. It didn't matter. Going by feel alone, he was able to step off the ledge onto the top of the wall, and then, finally, lower himself to the cement floor.

The layout of the girls' shower room was similar to the boys'. Herb knew where all the light switches were, and he flooded the place with a bright yellow glow. He felt better immediately. He had never cared for the dark.

Before plugging in his extension cord, Herb cleaned up the glass and twisted metal from the fallen window. There was a broom and dustpan in the cage. He put the garbage in a can that stood in full view of everyone, but covered the mess with a pile of newspapers. Then he checked out the socket Sammie had told him about. Its location was excellent. It was at the back of the cage, at the top. The ledge that ran beneath the window ended not six feet above it. The only tricky part that he could see was where the cord would have to come over the ledge and into the cage. For those few feet, the cord would be exposed. There was no helping it.

Ten minutes later Herb had the extension cord in place and the VCR running. He had already decided how to program the shots—eight shots every four minutes, starting at 4:00 P.M. He did not feel a test shot was necessary. The setup was so simple, nothing could go wrong.

Unless they hear the clicking of the camera.

Herb was more worried about the sound of the camera than the VCR. The VCR would be in the back of the ledge, out of sight, but the camera had to be near the front edge. Plus a camera shutter made a very distinctive click. Heads usually turned when a camera was operating. Yet, he reasoned, the water should be running at that point. It should be OK.

Now Herb had to decide where to focus the camera. With his luck he would end up shooting the north end of the showers while the girls were splashing naked on the south end. He finally decided to aim the camera toward the center of the showers and adjust the lens so that he had the widest possible angle on the shot. It seemed a wise compromise. He would be sacrificing detail, but he could always blow up the shots later.

Herb climbed back down and surveyed his setup from ground level. The VCR was not visible from any point in the showers. Even the camera was not entirely out in the open. He had been able to use a portion of one of the plates that fastened the air compressor to hide half of it, and the other half he had obscured with a small empty jar he found. In fact, unless someone was to stare directly at the corner, and study it, she wouldn't know there was a camera there at all. The extension cord wrapping down toward the cage was not so carefully hidden, yet it looked harmless. No one would stop to yank on it in the next twenty-four hours, he was convinced.

Herb felt a surge of power. Several things had gone wrong already. Several more could yet go wrong. Still, he had a feeling that he was going to have his pictures, and that they were going to be great.

Herb turned off the lights and left the shower

room. He didn't go out the window. He used the
front door.

He was about to climb in his car when he heard
what he thought were footsteps. It was difficult to
pinpoint where they were coming from, but it
seemed to be somewhere near the center of campus. He strained his eyes to look through the dark
but saw nothing. No janitors worked that late, and
he was trying to rationalize what else could be
making the noise. A loose window banging in the
wind perhaps, even though there was no wind to
speak of. That did nothing to reassure him or his
nerves. *They* might be watching him now, knowing
he was trying to watch them. He wondered if he
should try to find out who it was, or if he should
jump in his car and make a run for it. But he
made a typical Herb Trasker decision, which was
to decide to do nothing. He just stood there in
the dark, listening. The sound never returned,
and eventually he convinced himself he had just
imagined it.

His calm only lasted until he was in his car and
driving across the school parking lot to the exit. It
was when he spotted Theo slumped over the wheel
of his car in the corner of the lot that an ice-cold
needle of fear stabbed Herb in the chest. Theo was
dead, he thought.

The pain eased a few seconds later when Herb
pulled up beside his friend. Theo had merely
passed out at the wheel, waiting for him. That's
what he said, anyway.

"What are you doing here?" Herb demanded, wondering if Theo had followed him to the girls' showers and watched him climb the tree with the VCR.

"I followed you here," Theo said.

"Why? I thought you were getting something to eat."

"I lost my appetite." Theo rubbed his tired eyes. "Where's Alexa?"

"I don't know. Home in bed, I suppose."

"You didn't meet her here?"

"No."

Theo sat up and glanced across the lot, in the direction of the gymnasium and the showers. "Then why are *you* here?"

"I lost my lens cap this afternoon while I was photographing the cheerleaders. I wanted to look for it before some jerk swiped it." Herb was pleased at how easily the lie came to him. Ordinarily he lied about as well as a politician.

"Did you find it?" Theo asked.

"Yeah." Herb paused. "I didn't see you follow me here."

Theo smiled. "I was sneaky about it."

Herb continued to feel uneasy. "You weren't walking in the center of campus a few minutes ago, were you?"

"No. I passed out here." It was Theo's turn to pause. "Why? Did you hear someone?"

"I thought I did."

"Maybe it was Alexa."

Herb had to laugh. "Maybe." He put his car in gear. "I've got to go home. I'm bushed."

"Think you'll make it into school tomorrow?" Theo asked.

"I hope so. There's some stuff I want to pick up."

CHAPTER FIVE

Herb didn't make it to first period. In fact, it was close to noon before he woke. For a long time he just lay in bed, enjoying the rest, not aware that he was about to embark upon the most traumatic day of his life.

When he did finally saunter into the kitchen, he saw that his mother had been up extra early and gone to the store. The icebox was now jammed with food—there had been little to eat when he had gotten home that morning. Herb wasn't a big eater, though, and when he did try to gain a few pounds by stuffing himself, he just felt sick. Sitting at the kitchen table, he had a bowl of cornflakes and a glass of apple juice. He started on the paper. It was not unusual for Herb to read the paper from front to back. He also enjoyed magazines, but he'd never been much of a book person. Books got too complicated for him. He'd usually just flip to the last page to see what happened.

It was two o'clock before Herb finished the newspaper and his cornflakes. By then there was no point in going to class. He didn't fret about what he'd missed, even though he had a vague recollection that there was supposed to have been an important test in English. He went into the living room and plugged an old movie into the VCR. He had watched the movie before, but since he couldn't remember the ending, he didn't mind watching it again. It was about giant mutant ants that ate policemen and little girls. He thought the special effects were excellent.

Around five o'clock he began to think about driving by Alexa's house. He knew it was a crazy idea—like she would just happen to be outside when he drove by. There was no way he was going to stop and knock on her door. Still, he thought there might be a tiny chance she'd be outside watering the front lawn. Her house had a nice lawn. He hadn't noticed a sprinkler system, so someone must water it. He didn't have anything to do anyway. Work didn't start until six. To be on the safe side, he couldn't pick up his camera and the film until the middle of the night. He decided to give it a shot, and figured he could always drive through McDonald's afterward if he didn't see her. Maybe she'd be there having a shake and fries.

Herb had left Mannville proper and was heading into the heights, when he saw the smoke. At first he thought it was from a truck. It was gray, like oil exhaust, and there wasn't much of it. But then the thin plume of smoke suddenly transformed into a black billow, as fat as a pregnant cloud. Herb put his foot down on the gas. The rainfall had been light the previous winter. The prickly shrubs that chewed the sides of Mannville's hills were ready to ignite. If a fire got going, it would do a lot of damage before it was put out.

The smoke was not so close as it initially appeared. Herb had to drive another mile into the hills before he found the source. A car had gone off the side of a cliff at a sharp bend in the road. After parking his Mustang on the shoulder, Herb recognized the spot and figured the person or people in the car had to be dead. He didn't have to walk to the edge of the cliff and look down—it was the same spot where Roger, Theo's brother, had been killed. Herb knew the drop to the bottom of the cliff was over three hundred feet.

Yet Herb walked to the edge and looked down anyway. It was an ugly sight, but fascinating. The car, a red Fiat, was completely engulfed in flames. The vehicle had hit the rock below head-on, and the gas tank had probably exploded on impact. Both the front and rear ends had totally disintegrated. The fire was fierce. Herb could barely hear the roar of air as it sucked through the shattered windows and fed the orange blaze above the sound of his own blood crashing in his ears. He recognized the car. It belonged to Stephen Plead, Alexa's boyfriend.

But was Stephen driving?

Herb couldn't tell from where he was standing. All he could see was that there had been only one person, the driver, in the car. He would have to climb down to the bottom to know more.

Herb glanced up and down the road, looking for help. There was no one in sight. It was another cooker of a day. The sweat poured off his forehead as the rising smoke from the burning car stung his eyes. He was hot all right, yet suddenly in the center of his spine he became icy cold. He felt that if he climbed down into the gorge he might not make it back out. Suddenly the gorge seemed to be a vast haunted graveyard, where the ghosts of the dead clamored for company. Roger Corbin was very much on his mind then. Herb couldn't see who was behind the wheel, but he could tell that the person was small.

A girl maybe.

He had to know. Against his better judgment he decided to climb to the bottom. But first he had to walk back down the road a quarter of a mile. There was no path, but the place where he stepped off the road was less cluttered with shrubs and dead grass, and the pseudotrail continued on down to the bottom, cutting at a sharp angle against the side of the cliff. Fortunately for the surroundings, the floor of the gorge where the car had crashed was pretty much solid rock. There was nothing handy to burn.

Except flesh.

It was definitely a girl. A white girl turning black. The heat of the blaze forced Herb to halt forty feet from the car. The girl was not sitting comfortably. The force of the impact had rammed her head into the car ceiling. Her clothes and hair were gone, and her skin was going fast. Herb tried to look away but the sight held him locked in a sick hold. Thoughts of hell and eternal damnation spun in his brain. He tried to tell himself that she was dead, that she had died on impact, yet he had to wonder if that was true.

Maybe she had felt everything.

The fire looked so clean, so purifying, but the black stinking smoke it spun off as it transformed layer after layer of bloody flesh into filthy ash told Herb it was a fire from below. His fear up on the cliff returned sharply. The food in his stomach welled up in his throat. The girl's face was nothing more than that of a mummy's—a mummy that had fallen into a vat of corrosive acid. Yet somehow Herb was able to recognize her. It may have been because he had photographed her so carefully the day before.

It was Lisa Barnscull.

Herb turned away and vomited.

CHAPTER SIX

Time had gone by, but Herb wasn't sure exactly how much. There were people on the scene now. One of them was Alexa. Another was Sammie. Herb didn't know where they had come from. He was sitting on a rock about a hundred yards from the fried car. He had stumbled over and collapsed on it after he had made his mess on the ground. The fire was out. A couple of cops and firemen had arrived and sprayed it with white dust. They were late—the flames had been dying out anyway. From where he was sitting in the gorge, Herb could see an ambulance parked at the edge of the cliff overhead. A plastic-gloved paramedic was slowly easing what was left of Lisa out of the wreckage.

He should have brought a dustpan with him.

Herb watched as Sammie broke away from the cops and firemen and walked toward him. He knew one of the cops wouldn't be far behind her.

"Did you see how it happened?" Sammie asked. Incredibly, she had a huge wad of gum in her mouth and was busy chewing away. Yet it would have been a mistake to say she looked unaffected. Her hand trembled visibly as she raised it to brush her shaggy hair off her face.

"No," Herb said flatly.

"Then what are you doing here?" Sammie asked.

"I was driving by, I saw the smoke." He shrugged. "What are you doing here?"

"The same."

"Did you come with Alexa?"

"Huh? No. Why would I do that?" she questioned shrilly.

"I don't know." He paused. "It is definitely Lisa, right?"

"Everyone seems to think so. The police got Stephen on their radio. He says he loaned Lisa his Fiat."

Herb nodded in the direction of Alexa. She was conferring with the police. As far as Herb could tell she had not once turned her eyes in the direction of the exploded car. She looked as white as a pale moon. "How did she end up here?" Herb asked.

"She was probably just driving home," Sammie said. "I don't think the police called her." Sammie stared at the wreckage. "Lisa's not going to be voted prom queen this year."

"Sammie," Herb protested.

"Well, I'm sorry, but she was a jerk."

Herb stood. "I'm happy she won't be bothering you anymore."

Sammie was insulted. "You didn't like her either."

"She wasn't so bad. She might have turned out to be nice." Herb thrust his hands in his pockets and bowed his head. "I wish she'd had the chance."

The bigger of the two cops broke away from the group and walked toward Herb and Sammie. He had a red face, like that of a man who enjoyed his whiskey, and a bulging gut that looked well muscled. His expression was dark—appropriate for the circumstances—but he looked as if he were ordinarily a cheerful man. Someone who could visit the scene of a tragic accident in the afternoon, and still enjoy the company of his grandchildren in the evening. He nodded to Herb and offered his hand. Apparently he had already made Sammie's acquaintance.

"I'm Sergeant Fitzsimmons," he said. "I understand you're Herb Trasker?"

Herb shook the cop's hand and was surprised at how gentle the man's grip was. "That's right," Herb said.

"Would it be all right if I ask you a few questions?"

"Sure."

"You were the first one to reach the scene of the accident?"

"Yeah."

"What did you see?"

Herb fidgeted. "The same thing you see now. Except the fire was burning then."

"Was there anyone around when you first got here?"

"No."

"How did you know the car was down here?"

"I saw the smoke. I drove straight here."

"Did you hear the sound of the crash?"

"I was about a mile from here when I saw the smoke—on the other side of the hill. I didn't hear anything."

"How long would you say it was between when you arrived here and the car went off the cliff?"

"I don't know. Five minutes. It's hard to say."

Fitzsimmons turned to stare at the empty wreck. The paramedic had managed to get Lisa out of the car. He was laying her out inside a plastic green bag. The three of them watched as the paramedic pulled up the zipper and Lisa disappeared for good from the face of the earth. Herb felt his eyes moisten and lowered his head to study the ground near his feet. The police officer noticed.

"She was a friend of yours?" Fitzsimmons asked.

In a way, yeah. That's my vomit over there.

"Sort of," Herb said. "We both knew her."

"She was a cheerleader at our school," Sammie added.

Fitzsimmons sighed. "I understand she was a beautiful girl."

"Yeah," Herb said. "She was very pretty. I took some pictures of her yesterday."

Fitzsimmons gestured to Alexa. "That girl over there says she was her best friend. Is that true?"

"Yeah," Herb said.

"She wants to accompany us back to the station and await the results of the autopsy," Fitzsimmons said. "She wants you to come with her."

"Me?" Herb said, surprised.

"Yes," Fitzsimmons said. "Do you want to come?"

"All right," Herb said.

"Why are you doing an autopsy?" Sammie asked.

Fitzsimmons studied Sammie. "We usually do one to find out the cause of death."

"But she died in the car crash," Sammie said.

"But why did her car crash?" Fitzsimmons said.

Sammie wiped her upper lip and raised her eyes to the top of the cliff. "It's a sharp turn in the road. Lisa always did drive like a maniac."

"But she drove this road every day of her life," Herb said, studying the cliff and remembering how well Roger had known the road as well.

The police station was not in Mannville but in Parvo, a town four times the size of Mannville, located about twenty miles southwest of it. Herb drove his Mustang to Parvo with Alexa sitting by his side, and Sammie trailing them in her car. Sammie had insisted on accompanying them, which Herb couldn't understand. Fitzsimmons hadn't seemed to mind, though. Fitzsimmons acted as if everyone were welcome. He was in his black and white, a hundred yards in front of them and not far behind the ambulance that carried Lisa's remains.

"She always liked Fridays," Alexa said suddenly. They were the first words she had spoken since she had climbed in his car twenty minutes earlier.

"She seemed like someone who enjoyed the weekends," Herb said, feeling stupid. Alexa just shook her head.

"She didn't like the weekends. Just Friday. Just the promise of the weekends. The reality never lived up to the promise for Lisa. It was always a disappointment to her."

"Why?" Herb asked. "She had lots of friends."

"I was her only friend." Alexa turned away and stared out the window. "Besides, she was right, they always *were* disappointing."

"I don't understand."

"It doesn't matter."

"This must be terrible for you," Herb said.

Alexa continued to stare out the window. "I don't know if I feel anything. Maybe I'm in shock. But I do have a feeling that something bad is about to happen, that it's going to hit soon—but I already know what it is. It's already happened. Lisa's dead. My friend is dead." Alexa shook her head. "But it's like I'm the dead one, and don't really know it, not yet."

"Is there anything I can do to help?"

Alexa turned her head toward him. Her huge green eyes were arresting. He had to struggle to keep his attention on the road. Her dark hair flowed over her white blouse, touching her white pants. She was all in white, and the lines around her wide mouth seemed to be traced in black by contrast. Her response caught him by surprise.

"You help me just by being here," she said.

"I don't know about that."

"You do. When I reached the scene of the accident, I couldn't look at what had happened. But just seeing you sitting alive on that rock made it all the more bearable." Alexa reached over and touched his knee. "I really mean that."

Herb smiled faintly, uncomfortably. "Thanks."

Alexa took her hand back and stared straight ahead. Her lower lip trembled. "I heard Sammie asking the policeman, but I didn't hear the answer —why do they have to do an autopsy?"

"I think they want to make sure it was an accident."

Alexa frowned. "Don't they think it was an accident?"

"Yeah. I think it's just routine."

"What do they do in an autopsy? Do you know? Exactly?"

Herb had read a thing or two about them, but didn't feel like going into the details. "I think they take tissue samples, do X-rays—stuff like that."

Alexa wasn't buying it. "They'll cut her open,

won't they? They'll cut out her brain. That's what they do in movies when they do one."

"Try not to think about it."

Alexa's whole face trembled this time. "She was so pretty."

"Yeah."

Alexa smiled faintly, biting her lower lip. "We were both so vain. We'd always tell each other that we were the prettiest girls in the school, and laugh at how ugly everyone else was. We'd do that right before we'd get in a fight about who *was* the prettiest—her or me. I always said I was, and you can imagine what Lisa said." Alexa glanced at him. "Dumb, huh?"

"It sounds like a normal friendly argument."

She lost her smile. "It wasn't always so friendly. We weren't always nice to each other. I told you that the other day." Alexa hesitated. "Maybe I should have been nicer to her. Maybe it would have made a difference, you know, with what happened today."

"You can't blame yourself. That would be crazy."

"I am to blame—in a way. I should have given her a ride home. She shouldn't have had to borrow Stephen's car. She always drove too fast in that thing."

Again Herb was struck by how Stephen seemed to have been Lisa's boyfriend, rather than Alexa's. "If you'd been with her, you both might have died," he said.

"Do you think that's possible?"

He shrugged. "I'm no philosopher."

Alexa was interested. "You see, I don't think that's possible. I feel like I'm never going to die. Does that sound crazy? I mean, I know I have a body, that it's going to wear out, but I just can't see it happening." Then she stopped herself. "But I suppose Lisa felt the same way." She looked at him out of the corner of her eye. "You're a nice boy, Herb, did anyone ever tell you that?"

"My mom."

"Your mom is right. What's she like?"

Herb shrugged. "She's nice. What's yours like?"

"I don't know. She never talks to me."

"Do you two fight?"

"No, we don't do anything. We simply coexist."

"That's too bad. How about your dad?"

"Don't even ask about him."

"I'm sorry."

"It doesn't bother me," Alexa said. "Lisa never got along with her parents, either. She hated them, in fact. I could see why. They were awful." Again Alexa stopped herself. "Do you think I'm being bitchy?"

"Of course not," Herb said.

"No, I mean seriously. Sometimes I do things that hurt people, and I ask myself why I did that. But the next day I'll do the same thing all over again."

"What have you ever done that's hurt someone?"

"You'd be amazed." Alexa thought for a moment. "What do you think the autopsy will show?"

Herb was confused. "What do you mean?"

"I mean if I haven't always been a nice girl, Lisa was sometimes a bad girl."

"Do you think she was drinking and driving?"

Alexa snorted softly. "That would hardly be the beginning of it."

Alexa fell silent, and Herb didn't question her further. After a while Alexa began to cry softly, and still Herb didn't speak. It broke his heart to hear Alexa in pain, but he knew he couldn't do anything to take it away.

The station in Parvo was new—all red brick and white paint. Fitzsimmons led Herb and Alexa inside, and Sammie jumped out of her car and scurried in after them. Yet Sammie maintained her behavior of the previous day, trying to pretend Alexa wasn't there. Alexa also ignored Sammie, only pausing at the threshold of the station to ask Sammie what she was doing there.

"I just want to see what happened," Sammie said.

They went inside. Fitzsimmons had them sit in his office. It was small and cluttered and smelled of air freshener. Fitzsimmons had failed to reach Lisa's parents. Alexa told him that they probably had already left for a weekend visit to San Francisco. She wasn't sure which hotel they were staying at. Fitzsimmons pressed her to remember. They needed Lisa's parents' permission to perform the autopsy. He told them once again it was unnecessary for them to be there at all. Yet he said it without conviction, and Herb received the impression that he wanted to keep an eye on them until he had the facts clear in his own mind.

Alexa remembered the name of the hotel after a bit.

CHAPTER SEVEN

In the End

"Did you think I was suspicious?" Fitzsimmons asked.

"I didn't know what you were doing," Herb said.

"Alexa wanted to see what the autopsy showed. Did she tell you that?"

"I think Alexa already knew what it was going to show," Herb replied.

"That's what you implied. How could she know?"

"She was Lisa's best friend," Herb said. "I'm sure she knew Lisa took cocaine."

"Lisa took a lot of cocaine. She had taken a lot over a long period of time. We didn't tell you that at the station."

"You didn't tell me anything. Alexa told me about her drug habit."

"We couldn't," Fitzsimmons said. "You understand. It was private information. The only reason

Alexa found out was because she said it straight to my face in my office right after I received the results from the coroner. It was so late at night then that I saw no point in denying it."

"Yeah."

"Herb, can I ask you something? Who do you think it was at school the night you planted the camera?"

"It could have been any of them—Sammie, Theo, Alexa. Maybe it was Stephen, I don't know."

"You don't think it was Lisa?"

"No," Herb said.

"Why not?"

"Because she died at the beginning."

"What do you mean by that remark?" Fitzsimmons asked.

Herb paused. "Nothing. I just said it."

"Tell me when Sammie and Alexa arrived at the scene of the crash."

"I don't know," Herb said. "I was spacing out. Didn't they come after you got there?"

"They were standing at the edge of the road when we drove up. They were together, but it appeared they had come in separate cars. You honestly don't know when they got there?"

"I have no idea."

"Was that your vomit?"

"It wasn't Lisa's," Herb said.

"Sorry. You already told me that you didn't hear the sound of the car as it crashed. My next question's going to sound silly, but I have to ask it. Did you hear any squeal of tires?"

"No. I was too far away."

"Lisa didn't put on the brakes before she went off the ledge."

"There weren't any skid marks?" Herb asked.

"Only old ones."

"It doesn't surprise me."

"Because Lisa was loaded?" Fitzsimmons asked.

"I have to finish my story. It'll explain that. But maybe you can tell me how loaded she was? And how could the coroner tell anyway? I thought she was burned pretty bad."

"Drug toxicity is determined by a blood test," Fitzsimmons said. "Lisa was badly burned but it was still possible to get a blood sample from her. From our tests, I can tell you she was loaded at the time her car crashed. But how loaded—from her perspective—I can't say. Someone who takes cocaine regularly can snort a tremendous amount and appear relatively clearheaded."

"What test made you think she was a long-time user?"

"The cartilage inside her nose survived. The coroner said that Lisa must have been snorting cocaine on a regular basis for at least a year. The cartilage was badly damaged."

"Her nose always looked OK from the outside," Herb said.

"Cocaine is for the most part a functional drug. She could have been high as a kite and still gone to school." Fitzsimmons stopped for a moment. He may have been writing something down, Herb decided. "Do you know if Alexa shared her friend's habit?"

"No."

"What about Sammie? Stephen?"

"Sammie wasn't into coke. I don't know about Stephen."

"And Theo?" Fitzsimmons asked.

"The hardest thing Theo ever took was beer."

"Did you take Alexa home after you left the station?"

"No. Sammie took her."

"I thought they didn't like each other?"

"They just went home together. I don't know whose idea it was. It might have been Sammie's."

"But didn't you want to take Alexa home? You told me how much you liked her."

"I didn't care. It was late."

"Where did you go after you left the station?"

"You know."

"You went for the film?"

"Yeah."

"Why? You must have had other things on your mind besides naked girls."

"I did." Herb hesitated. "I just had this feeling."

"What kind of feeling?"

"A feeling of dread."

CHAPTER EIGHT

But Herb's feeling of dread was buried deep as he stood on the dark campus beside the tall tree, under the open window. What dominated his conscious mind were confusion and excitement; the former because Lisa had been alive and pretty only a few hours earlier, and the latter because there was still the roll of film. The film that may hold either Lisa or Alexa, or both, naked together during their last minutes of friendship on planet Earth.

He was up and inside the window in minutes. He had his flashlight with him, and he saw in a flash that the VCR and the camera had not been disturbed. He worked his way immediately over to the corner ledge and then down onto the floor, where he reached for a light switch. He didn't want to work in the dark because he was suddenly afraid of it. He couldn't get Lisa's burnt remains out of his head. Yet his excitement anticipating his pictures remained. He thought he was some kind of a pervert.

"I mean . . . Lisa was sometimes a bad girl."

Had she really taken all those drugs? It was amazing he had never noticed. But then, he hadn't noticed the same thing about Roger. He wondered who had turned on whom. He wondered if Theo had heard about the accident.

Accident.

It was strange how funny the word sounded in his thoughts.

Like some kind of bad joke.

His feeling of dread took a brief peek at the surface.

Herb unplugged the extension cord and scaled the wall back up to the ledge with the cord. The height no longer bothered him—it was a lot less than the distance to the bottom of the gorge, he thought, and if he fell he wouldn't explode on impact. He wondered what it had felt like to fly through the air like that, in a red sports car, watching the ground rush toward you. She had probably screamed all the way to the bottom.

He checked the camera. It had taken eight pictures.

"It worked," he whispered.

He gathered his equipment up and climbed down to the floor again. It was only after he had flipped off the light and was going out the door that the thought of fingerprints crossed his mind. He stopped in the doorway and looked behind him into the dark. He was being paranoid. A few hundred girls went through those doors every day, touching everything in sight. Besides, he couldn't possibly remember everything he had touched to wipe clean.

There was another reason he didn't go back in and try to remove his prints from the window and ledge at least. It was dark in the showers. He knew all he had to do was turn on the light and the darkness would fly, but just peering into it made him want to go home and curl up under his blankets.

But who was he fooling? He wasn't going home to sleep. He was going to develop the film. As he raced toward his house, he mentally reviewed whether he had all the necessary chemicals. He figured in less than an hour, if all went according to plan, he should have fresh prints.

Herb's plans briefly crumbled when he reached his house and saw Theo's car parked in his driveway. Theo *must* have heard about Lisa and ditched work to come over and talk. What would Theo's mood be? Sympathetic? Pleased? A little of both?

Herb parked and left the equipment in the trunk of his car. He opened the front door gently. He could move quietly when it suited him because he came home late every night and never disturbed his mother. His stealth kept him from disturbing Theo, who had crashed on a living room chair, his head thrown back, his mouth wide open and sawing sequoias. Theo snored like a badly timed internal combustion engine. Herb knew that once asleep Theo was like a dead man. Herb went back to his car for his equipment. The night was still young, he thought, and full of promise.

Herb had a makeshift darkroom in his bedroom. Next to his camera, it was his pride and joy. Constructing it the previous spring had taken big bites out of his bimonthly paychecks. The most difficult part had been tapping into the bathroom plumbing and putting a sink and faucet in the corner of his room. The darkroom was not technically separate from his bedroom, but the black vinyl sheets he had draped from the ceiling effectively cut out all extraneous light. Herb removed the film from his camera and closed himself inside the corner. Quickly he reviewed what he had on hand. He was low on fixer, but figured he had just enough. He reached for the light switch.

The first step was to remove the film from the roll and place it in a spool, which prevented the film surfaces from touching. This had to be done in total darkness. Next he slipped the spool into a developing tank, clamping down a light-tight lid. Once he had the lid in place he was able to turn the light back on.

He used three chemicals to develop photographs: film developer, stop bath, and fixer. Film developer did what the name implied; it reacted with the film and imprinted the images the camera lens had recorded. Stop bath halted the developing process.

It was an acidic solution and smelled like vinegar. In fact, Herb's entire room smelled like vinegar. He was so used to it he hardly noticed anymore.

Fixer helped remove the other chemicals from the film. It made the images permanent. All the chemicals had to be kept in the temperature range of sixty-eight to seventy-five degrees Fahrenheit. They didn't work otherwise. He had forgotten how warm it had been lately. He took out his thermometer and discovered the chemicals were all over eighty degrees. It was only a minor mistake and one he could rectify quickly. He took the chemicals into the kitchen and stuck them in the icebox for a few minutes. That should do it, he thought. He hoped he hadn't waked Theo in the process.

Theo had shifted positions in the living room. In fact, now he was lying on the couch. That really blew Herb's mind, that Theo had sleepwalked in someone else's house.

Herb was back in his darkroom ten minutes later with cool chemicals. He got out his timer and set it to eight minutes. Quickly he poured the developer solution into the tank, filling it to the top. He capped it and inverted it several times. This was called agitating the solution, which was a fancy expression for making sure the stuff soaked over the film. Several times he tapped the tank on his counter to dislodge any bubbles. He did this for exactly eight minutes, but slowed as he went along, until at the end he was hardly shaking the tank at all. When the timer reached zero, he uncapped the tank and poured the solution down the drain.

Next he added stop bath to the tank, again recapping it. Here the timing was not so critical. He shook it for about a minute before pouring the solution away.

Herb remembered he had bought a bottle of Rapid Fix a couple of months earlier. Rapid Fix was often used by newspaper photographers when they were in a hurry to make a deadline. It cut the fix phase from ten minutes down to two. Incredibly, Herb remembered exactly where he had put the bottle—under his work counter. He poured a quarter of the bottle into the tank and let it soak the film for the brief time. Then he threw the solution away.

Now Herb had to rinse the film in water. Many photographers used distilled water for this step, but Herb was not a purist and couldn't afford to be fussy. He held the tank containing the film—with the cap off—under his faucet with the water running. A good wash lasted twenty minutes. The water further removed the chemicals from the film so they wouldn't stain it and shorten the life of the film. But Herb was in a hurry so he let the film wash for only ten minutes. It wouldn't matter that much anyway.

He was now ready to remove the film from the tank. Ordinarily at this stage he would let the film sit for an hour and dry. But he had another method to hurry the process—his mother's hair dryer. When he was through with it—two minutes later —he got ready to cut the dried film into strips. Here he deviated somewhat from his normal method. With a roll of thirty-six exposures, he would cut it in six strips of six. But that night he just cut off the first eight shots as a whole, and set the other twenty-eight unused exposures aside. He laid the eight out on his light table, a narrow work space topped with translucent glass that covered a row of four tiny lights. Then he reached for his loupe—a small magnifier.

Few laypeople understood that a negative contained far more detail than a print could ever show. For most people a negative was just a blur of lines and shadows. But as Herb bent over the negatives, with his loupe in hand, he was in position to see exactly what there was to see.

Oh, God.

Herb almost fainted.

There was nobody in the first four negatives, and only one girl in the next three. It was Lisa, standing in the showers in the last twelve minutes of his exposures—standing fully exposed. Herb studied her, fascinated. She had a hell of a body, and Herb had seen enough playmates of the month to make a value judgment. The shots had caught her from a variety of angles: front, side, behind—she had the cutest ass. But none of those were what made Herb want to faint. It just made him feel a little sick, to realize what was to become of her less than an hour after the pictures were taken.

It was the last shot that really got him.

The last shot with two people in it.

The shot of someone with a baseball bat creeping toward Lisa.

The someone who looked like a fully clothed Alexa Close.

CHAPTER NINE

Herb stepped from his darkroom and sat on the edge of his bed for a long time. He didn't spend the time entertaining profound thoughts. Only a single stupid question kept floating around in his brain—something about Alexa's batting average. He had never even known she liked baseball. Yeah, he just sat there and let the smell of the vinegar stop bath gel his brain cells. Finally, though, he stood and reentered the darkroom. His work wasn't done yet. He thought if he kept himself busy enough, long enough, he wouldn't ever have to think about the baseball bat and what Alexa had done with it. He was a master of self-deception. From birth, he had convinced himself that there was a wonderful reason for all the horrible things God allowed to happen in the world.

Herb cut out the eighth negative and inserted it into a negative holder, which he then placed into his enlarger. He flipped on his safelight and flipped off the overhead one. The safelight glowed a dull reddish orange, making him think he could be on Mars. He turned on the enlarger and focused it onto his easel. The easel held the paper on which the print would be made. He focused the image to a size of eight-by-eleven. Pretty standard. Then he turned off the light inside the enlarger and took out his photograph paper, contained in a light-tight box. He inserted the paper into the easel and set the enlarger timer for ten seconds. When the timer reached ten seconds, the enlarger light automatically went off. The image on the negative had now been burned onto the paper.

Herb removed the paper from the easel and put it in his developer tray, which was filled with Dektol, a common developer. He gently stirred it around for a minute, and in that sixty seconds the picture fully formed before his eyes. Nothing had changed. Lisa was still in the shower, and Alexa was still approaching her with bat in hand.

Herb put the print in the stop bath for thirty seconds, then the fixer for another two minutes. Finally he washed the print in water and set it down on a bunch of paper towels. He blotted up the moisture without care. He wanted to blot out what he was looking at.

He felt so confused.

Alexa could not have murdered Lisa, he thought. That would mean Alexa *was* a murderer. But Alexa was a cheerleader, and Lisa was a cheerleader. No, that wasn't right. Lisa was a *dead* cheerleader. She was ashes. She was smoke. She had snorted one gram of cocaine too many and burned out the inside of her skull, before she drove off the face of a wicked cliff and caught on fire at the bottom.

It was the drugs, Herb kept telling himself. She had been high and made a wrong turn—just like poor Roger. But Herb would have had to be high to believe it. The truth may have come to him slowly, but when it did come, it hit with a wallop.

Alexa smashed in Lisa's head in the shower. Then she dragged Lisa out to the Fiat, drove her up to the cliff, and rolled her over the edge.

Several things happened almost at once then.

The phone in Herb's bedroom rang.

Someone knocked at the front door.

Theo stopped snoring and mumbled.

Herb flipped on his regular light and reached for the phone.

"Hello?" he said.

"Herb, it's me. I've got to talk to you."

"Alexa? What are you doing? How come you're not in bed?" He glanced at the clock beside his bed. "It's one in the morning."

"Are you alone?"

"No. I was a second ago. I think there's someone at the door. And Theo's here."

"Who's at the door? What's Theo doing there?"

"Theo was asleep on my couch when I got home. I don't know who's at the door."

Alexa spoke urgently. "It's probably Sammie. Get rid of her, then call me right back."

"What's wrong?" It was incredible but for a moment he had forgotten all about the picture he had just developed. When he did remember, though, he didn't feel comfortable talking to Alexa on the phone. The person at the front door knocked again. Herb could hear Theo getting up and asking who it was.

"I can't explain right now," Alexa said. "I think Lisa was murdered. It's crucial that I see you right away."

"Murdered?" Herb said. "What makes you think that?"

Alexa paused. "You better get the door."

"All right."

"Then call me right back. It's five-five-two-two."

Herb wrote down the four numbers. Every number in Mannville began with four-seven-two. "All right."

Herb hung up the phone and went into the living room. Theo had already opened the door to let Sammie in. Sammie looked anxious. Theo looked drunk. Herb noticed for the first time the cans of beer beside the chair where Theo had originally been.

"That bitch got fried," Theo mumbled, sagging against the wall, unable to support himself.

"Don't say that," Herb said. "What are you doing here? What are you both doing here?"

"Herb?" his mother called from her room at the end of the hall.

"It's just Sammie and Theo," Herb called back. "They're leaving."

"I have to talk to you, Herb," Sammie said nervously.

Theo belched. "She burned. She's hamburger now."

"How many beers have you had?" Herb asked him.

Theo gestured to the litter beside the chair. "How many are there?"

"You've got to go home," Herb said to Theo. "Sammie, drive him home. I can't talk to anybody right now."

"Theo," Sammie said. "Go out and get in my car. I'll be out in a few minutes."

"Roger got her," Theo said, slurring his words. "I knew he would. Roger paid her back in full."

"So you're happy Lisa's dead," Herb said, disgusted.

Theo grinned stupidly. "I'm content." He turned around and walked into the wall. Then he stumbled toward the door. "Where's my gun? I brought my gun."

"I think I saw it outside on the front lawn," Sammie said, shifting uneasily from leg to leg. "Go get it, Theo. Just wait for me by my car."

"Why did you bring your gun?" Herb asked as Theo stumbled out onto the porch. Theo tried to turn and answer but didn't make it. He tripped off a step and landed facedown on the grass. Sammie closed the door on him.

"What's with you?" Herb asked.

"I drove Alexa home, you know," Sammie said. "She was acting strange. I have to talk to you about it."

"What do you mean by strange? Her best friend just died. Is she supposed to act normal?"

"Why are you yelling at me?"

Herb thought it was a weird question. He was talking in a moderate tone. "I'm not yelling at you. I'm just tired. I want to go to bed."

Sammie glanced toward his bedroom. The glow from his safelight was visible even with the overhead light on. "Are you developing pictures?"

"No."

"Why do you have your safelight on?"

"Look, can't this wait until tomorrow? I'm really tired."

Sammie took a step toward his bedroom. "You did take the pictures of the cheerleaders in the showers. Let me see them. I have to see them."

"Why?"

Sammie whirled on him. "You did take them!"

"Shh. You already said that. Yeah, so what? I took a bunch of pictures of empty showers."

"Why won't you let me see them then?"

"I haven't printed them yet," Herb said.

"Are you sure? You're lying. You wouldn't have the safelight on unless you were printing. I'll wait until you're done."

"You have to take Theo home."

"To hell with Theo. He's probably asleep on the lawn by now."

"Herb," Mrs. Trasker called.

"She's just leaving," Herb called back. He spoke to Sammie. "Why are you so eager to see those pictures?"

"What pictures? You just said you hadn't even printed them yet."

"You're not answering my question," Herb said.

"You're not answering mine," Sammie snapped back. "What time did you set your exposures for?"

"Four o'clock, just like you told me." Herb stopped. It was an amazing coincidence, even to someone like him, that he should have just happened to catch Lisa and Alexa in such a delicate position. When he spoke next, he was whispering. "Why did you tell me four o'clock?"

Sammie took a step back and lowered her head. "Because that's when they usually take their showers."

"I see. What do you mean Alexa was acting strange?"

"She was talking about Lisa like she didn't like her."

"I don't believe that," Herb said.

Sammie glanced back toward his bedroom. "You're hiding something from me. Who just called?"

"No one."

"I was standing on the front porch when the phone rang. Was it Alexa who called?"

"No."

"Who then?"

"It was a wrong number. What exactly did Alexa say?"

It was Sammie's turn to play ignorant. "Stuff."

"What kind of stuff?"

Sammie became defiant. She raised her fat chin. "Stuff that made me think she might have killed Lisa."

Herb snorted. "Right, Alexa killed Lisa and then admitted it to you. Why would she do that?"

"I didn't say she admitted it. I said she was acting weird." Sammie started to push by him, to get to the bedroom. Herb grabbed her arm. Sammie angrily shook free. "Are you going to let me see them or not?" she demanded.

"There's nothing to see," Herb said flatly.

Sammie glared at him. "I might go to the police, you know."

Now Herb felt angry. "And tell them what?"

Sammie shook her head, beginning to move toward the front door. "What you did was illegal. You could get in a lot of trouble."

"If I do, so will you."

"Yeah, well, thanks for nothing." Sammie opened the door and glanced outside. "Theo's gone."

"I guess he drove himself home," Herb said, standing behind her and scanning the front lawn.

"I doubt he makes it. Goodbye, Herb," she said and slammed the door in his face.

"Great," Herb muttered to himself.

He returned to his bedroom and dialed Alexa's number. She answered on the first ring. She sounded upset, but still very much in control.

"I think I'm being set up for Lisa's murder," she said right away.

"Was Lisa murdered?" Herb asked.

"No," Alexa said. "At least I don't think so. I thought she had just snorted too much coke and mixed up turning right with turning left. But I found a note on my desk in my room when I got home. It was in an envelope. It had my name on the outside. I'll read it to you. It says, 'We have pictures of what you did to Lisa.'"

"Do you know what it means?" Herb asked.

"No. I didn't do anything to Lisa. She was in a car crash. She was alone when she crashed." Alexa paused. "Do *you* know what it's about?"

Herb began to feel somewhat better. Unless Alexa knew about his pictures, which seemed unlikely, and was the most extraordinary liar in the world, she was probably innocent. On the other hand, if she was innocent, who had written the note? The person who had killed Lisa?

This is all just a sick joke. It has to be.

"Do you recognize the handwriting on the note?" Herb asked.

"It's typed."

"Was your mom home before we left for Parvo?"

"No," Alexa said. "And the place was unlocked. Anyone could have come in and left the note on my desk. Herb, what does this mean? What pictures?"

Herb chewed on the whole of his life for a moment. He was nothing to look at. He was kind of a loser. On the other hand, Alexa was gorgeous. She was witty. She was perfect. Plus he liked her, and he was beginning to get the idea that she liked him. The totally impossible was becoming the vaguely possible. They might end up dating. She might end up being his girlfriend. But if he told her he had set up his camera in the showers so that he could take nude pictures of her and the other cheerleaders, then she would think he was a pervert. It was a dilemma. He couldn't tell her the truth, yet he had to help her.

I'll tell her part of the truth.

"I have some pictures," he mumbled.

"What? Pictures of what?"

"Ah—pictures of you and Lisa."

"Do you mean the Sugar Sisters pictures? The pictures you took in the home ec room?"

"Not exactly."

Alexa sounded exasperated. "Herb, what pictures do you have?"

He cleared his throat. "I have a picture of Lisa taking a shower at school and you sneaking up on her with a baseball bat."

Alexa didn't say anything for an eternity. When

she finally did speak, her voice sounded strangely impressed. "You're kidding."

"No."

"Where did you get this picture? Did you take it?"

"No," he said quickly. "How could I?"

"Did it just fall into your lap?"

"No. Well, yeah, sort of. When I came home I found this roll of film in my bedroom." He added, "There was a note attached, like your note. It said for me to develop it."

"Herb, that sounds pretty lame."

"It's true," he said pitifully.

She took a breath. "I'm sorry, I'm not calling you a liar. I just don't know what's going on here. You understand. Is it just one picture?"

"There's only one that you're in," Herb said.

"Who's in the others?"

"Just Lisa."

"Is she naked in all of them?" Alexa asked.

"Well, she's taking a shower."

"Am I naked in the other one?"

"No. You have your clothes on."

Alexa snorted. "God, this is bizarre. Could you bring me the picture?"

"Now?"

"Yeah."

"Don't you think maybe we should take the picture and your note to the police?" Herb asked.

"No. Are you crazy? They'll take one look at that picture and think I killed Lisa and drove her up to the cliff and dumped her off. I have to see it before I can decide what to do. Bring it to me right now."

"All right."

"Have you made any extra prints?" Alexa asked.

"No, just the one."

"OK. I'll be waiting for you, Herb."

CHAPTER TEN

Herb took a shower before he left the house. It had been a long hot day and he stank. He brushed his teeth and shaved, too, even though he needed to shave about as much as an Eskimo needed a sunblock. He had never been a very hairy person. He put on a fresh pair of pants and a clean shirt. Then he returned to his bedroom and grabbed the incriminating photo of Alexa Close.

He didn't take the negative with him.

Herb hadn't thought through the entire matter. Vaguely, he still thought someone must be up to some nasty prank. He had not ruled out the possibility that it was Sammie or Theo, or even Alexa for that matter. He did not really think Lisa had been murdered. No one had ever been murdered in Mannville before. The odds should have been against someone he knew being the first one. Yet he was not ready to dismiss the entire idea. What he wanted to do was get more facts. He also wanted to see Alexa again. He was quite excited about the prospect. He sprayed deodorant under his arms before he took off for the front door.

He had the engine of his Mustang started and was just about to pull away, when his mother came out the door in her robe. She walked briskly over to him.

"Where are you going?" she asked, sounding slightly annoyed.

He turned the picture of naked Lisa upside down on the passenger seat. "I have to go over to Theo's house. I have to give him something."

"Can't it wait until tomorrow? It's almost two in the morning."

"No, it's important. I'm sorry we woke you up."

His mother threw worried glances up and down the street. "Does this have anything to do with that girl you called me about from Parvo? The one who died in that car crash?"

"No." He hated lying to his mother. She always knew when he was lying. She leaned over, resting her arms on the window.

"I want you to come back in the house and go to bed," she said.

"I can't."

"Why not? Call Theo and tell him you can't come."

"It's important, Mom."

"Wasn't he just here a few minutes ago?"

"It was more like a half-hour ago."

She stood up straight again, studying him closely. "You just washed your hair. You're going to see a girl."

He squeezed his steering wheel, staring at the garage door. "Yeah."

"Who is it?"

"Alexa Close."

"She's that girl you like?"

"Yeah."

"Wasn't it her best friend who died in the car crash?"

"Yes," Herb said. "Lisa Barnscull."

"Is Alexa having trouble dealing with it? Is that the reason you're going over?"

Herb looked up at his mother. "Yeah, she's very upset. I won't be gone long."

His mother sighed. "All right. I'll wait up till you come back."

"Don't. Please."

She turned and walked toward the front door. "I'll wait up lying in bed. If you're not back in an hour I'm going to come out looking for you."

He had to hope that she'd just pass out. She looked exhausted. It was strange how he no longer felt tired. In fact, he felt positively exhilarated. Lisa was dead and that was horrible, but Mannville hadn't seen so much action in a very long time.

Herb saw some action close up a few minutes later. He was on his way to the heights, almost to the road that Lisa had taken to her death, when he noticed he was being followed. He was sure it wasn't just somebody who happened to be going the same direction because the person had his headlights turned off—as if he were trying to be secretive. Even to Herb that seemed remarkably stupid.

Then his feelings on the matter changed. He was being followed by a blue Celica—Lisa's blue Celica. He was sure he had the right car, but in his rearview mirror, he couldn't see who was behind the wheel. He couldn't see if there was *anybody* behind the wheel. The idea that it *was* Lisa Barnscull occurred to him, followed by the even more disturbing possibility that Roger was with her. Herb liked to think he wasn't superstitious, but he was, in fact, a believer in most omens. The ghost possibility wouldn't go away, nor would the Celica. He speeded up and it speeded up. He turned right and it turned right. He began to sweat, ruining the effects of the shower he had taken especially for Alexa.

Herb managed to get himself back onto the main road that ran through Mannville, which at that time in the morning was about as crowded as a side street in Death Valley. It was his hope to make it to the Denny's at the far end of the strip. The coffee shop was always open, and sometimes a police officer stopped in for a late-night snack. Yet he had no sooner thought the words *police officer* than he began to feel paranoid.

What you did was illegal. You could get in a lot of trouble.

Only Herb could have simultaneously worried about two ghosts on his tail and a cop spotting his nude photo of a cheerleader. Only Herb would have stopped at a red light at two in the morning with a pursuer on his tail. No sooner did his Mustang come to a halt than the Celica swung up beside him. Someone big jumped out.

"Stephen," Herb said. He was so terrified to see the guy—even more terrified than if two decaying corpses had suddenly appeared to skin him alive—that his foot froze just above the accelerator. He was sitting like a duck posing for the barrel of a black shotgun. Stephen Plead easily reached his strong hand in through the window of Herb's Mustang and grabbed Herb by the collar.

"Where are they?" he demanded, pulling Herb six inches out of his seat.

"Who are they?" Herb was stupid enough to ask.

Stephen actually dragged Herb through the window and threw him facedown on the asphalt. When Herb tried to stand, Stephen slugged him in the gut. Herb didn't see the punch, he only felt as if a red-hot poker had been rammed into his diaphragm through a hole cut by a thick steel sword. The pain was so intense that Herb blacked out for a moment. The next thing he knew he was on the asphalt again, gasping for air that refused to enter his lungs. He felt as if his heart were going to rupture. More than anything in the world, he just wanted to be able to take a decent breath. He thought if he did, he'd be all right. He'd never have imagined Stephen was so strong.

Stephen, meanwhile, was chasing Herb's Mustang down the street. When Stephen had yanked him out the window, Herb hadn't put the car in park, or thrown on the parking brake. Herb had the Mustang idle set high to keep the car from stalling when he stopped at lights, and at that moment the car was trying to reach the Denny's without him.

Great. My car knows when to go for help.

The Mustang was only going five miles an hour, but even a slow-moving car is difficult to get into. Stephen first tried to reach inside and put on the brake. When that failed, he pulled open the door and jumped in. A moment later the car jerked to a halt and Herb heard Stephen swear.

"You little prick!" Stephen yelled.

Herb figured his punishment was not through. He tried to get up. Air still was not flowing freely into his lungs, but the knowledge that there were worse places Stephen could hit him gave him the strength to climb unsteadily to his feet. He turned in the direction of a closed Mobil station, always a wonderful place to hide in. He thought of making a run for it—and maybe constructing Molotov cocktails out of spare bottles and rags, and the sixty thousand gallons of gasoline in the underground tanks beneath the station—when he heard Stephen's hard boots rapidly approaching. His burning guts cried inside for him to do something—anything. He turned to face Stephen.

"I don't know nothing about that picture," he cried.

Stephen's face was a blur of unpleasantness. Yet his expression wasn't simply angry—it was crazed, as if he had gone for electroshock treatment at a nuclear power plant. The veins stood out from the sides of his neck like twisted cords. Stephen had the photo in one hand. He drew in a deep shuddering breath. Herb figured Stephen hadn't believed his lie.

"You are going to die," Stephen said.

Herb backed up a step, shaking. "I didn't take that picture."

Stephen took a step forward. "I am going to make you die."

"I don't even know where it came from. Please don't hurt me."

"You are going to die slowly."

Stephen leapt for him. Herb closed his eyes and screamed.

A shot rang out. A bullet ricocheted off the asphalt.

Herb opened his eyes.

Stephen had whirled all the way around and was now facing in the direction of the far-off Denny's. A car was approaching at high speed and a lunatic was hanging out the window with a rifle in one hand. The lunatic let off another shot, which sparked orange near Stephen's feet.

Theo.

Stephen may have been big, mean, and green, but he must have known how difficult bullets were to stop with muscle alone. He took off for Lisa's blue Celica, and Theo almost put a bullet in his foot before Stephen could jump behind the wheel. Herb enjoyed the sight of Stephen doing a skip in midair. But Stephen came close to mowing Herb down as he swung the Celica around and burned asphalt with stinking rubber.

He took my picture.

The Celica raced up the main road and vanished around a side street. Theo came to a halt beside Herb, still hanging out the window with his rifle in his left hand. Theo was laughing like a crazy man.

"Did I hit him?" he wanted to know.

"No. But you could have. You could have killed him. Are you nuts?"

"Wasn't he beating you up?" Theo asked, disappointed at Herb's reaction to being saved.

"Yeah. But you can't just shoot at people. Now he'll probably just find me tomorrow and beat me up twice as bad."

Theo set his rifle down inside his car. Herb noticed his own car had collided unharmed with the curb a hundred yards down the road. The right blinker had come on.

My car knows when to signal, too.

"I doubt that," Theo said.

"And what's that supposed to mean?" Herb demanded.

Theo ignored his question. He put his car in park and climbed out in the middle of the deserted road. "Why was he beating you up?"

"It must have been because of my going out with Alexa." Herb didn't draw a relationship between Alexa's call and Stephen's attack, even though Stephen was supposedly her boyfriend. Herb had told her he was bringing the photo right over. Why would she send an ape man to take what she was about to be handed?

"I thought you said you didn't go out with her," Theo said. He had sobered up considerably in the last half hour. Herb wondered if he'd really been that drunk.

"I was referring to when we went to McDonald's," Herb said.

"But you said that wasn't a date."

"I didn't explain it to Stephen, OK?" Herb stopped and gingerly fingered his abdomen. He figured he'd be pissing blood the next day, until he remembered his kidneys were in the back. He still hurt something fierce. "What are you doing out here at this time of night?" Herb asked.

"I was coming back to your house."

"Why?"

"After I'd had a couple cups of coffee, I remembered I forgot something."

"What?"

"My gun."

"But you have your gun."

"I know that," Theo said. "I noticed it was in the front seat beside me just before I saw Stephen belt you in the guts." Theo paused. "What was it he took out of your car?"

"What do you mean?"

"It was a piece of paper."

"I didn't see any piece of paper."

"It could have been a photograph."

"I don't know what you're talking about." Herb walked toward his car. "Thanks for saving my life, Theo, but you're beginning to give me a headache. I'm going home."

"By the way, what are *you* doing out here?" Theo called after him.

"Nothing!" Herb called back.

Herb climbed in his Mustang and made a U-turn in the center of the street. He was thankful Theo didn't chase after him.

That guy keeps showing up at the weirdest times.

Herb drove halfway home before deciding he had to go to Alexa's, picture or no picture. He'd just have to tell her the truth, that two ghosts in Lisa's Celica had stolen it. No, that wouldn't work. He'd tell her Stephen took it, but he'd leave out the part about Theo coming to his rescue. He had to maintain a little dignity in front of her.

On the road to Alexa's, he passed the spot where Lisa had gone skydiving. He didn't intend to stop. He certainly didn't mean to park and get out and look down at what was left of Stephen's car. But he did all of these things. He was Herb Trasker, and he didn't have control over his immediate environment, and that included his arms and his legs. Also, he just wanted to *peek*.

The red Fiat—no longer red but charcoal black now—was still there, snugged into the brown rock at the base of the gorge like some massive beetle that had been crushed. He wondered how much of Lisa was still there.

Herb checked his watch. It was now two-twenty. The night was never going to end. He turned away from the cliff and stepped back to his idling car. It was then that a cool layer of stagnant air brushed the right side of his face. Only it didn't feel like air exactly, but like a hand, a cold dead hand, and he jumped two feet off the ground before he could convince himself no one was there. No doubt about it, he thought, the place gave him the spooks.

Yet it hadn't always been that way. In fact, the hills just above the road had been a favorite spot for him and Sammie and Theo and Roger to hang out. That was in the good old days. It made Herb suddenly sad to be only eighteen years old and reminiscing about times lost and friends dead. The hill above the road climbed almost as steeply as the cliff fell, but it was free from prickly shrubs. It was made up mostly of smooth-faced boulders. They would sit on those huge rocks on the hill in the middle of the night and drink beer and look at the billion stars in the coal black sky. They used to talk for hours, about nothing usually.

Sometimes they got real corny. There was one night—it had been Roger's idea, he was full of fun—that they had hauled two five-gallon water bottles and a big bag of balloons up to their favorite boulder. It was about a hundred yards above the road. They met earlier that night than usual, about ten when cars were still going by. Their plan was to bomb the windshields of passersby.

"Maybe someone will come by on a motorcycle," Roger had said as they tied off the first balloons. "He'll think he's ridden into a thunderstorm."

"Nah," Theo had responded, holding the bottle for his brother. "No one's that dumb. He'll probably just drive off the road."

Roger had been suddenly concerned about that possibility, and later Herb was to wonder if a flash of premonition hadn't reached out from the future and touched Roger. "We'll try to hit them when they come out of the turn," he had said.

"We'll have to throw twice as far," Sammie had complained.

"That's all right," Roger said.

So they waited for the first car to come by, but it was a slow night and they had to sit awhile and drink beer, which kind of ruined their coordination. Finally a flatbed truck rolled by, but all they succeeded in doing was soaking the lumber on the back. Next came a station wagon filled with what looked like a four-square family. They plastered that sucker, and the father roared away as if he were under siege from artillery fire.

It was good fun. Roger changed his aim from windshields to drivers' windows—if they were down. That was fun for a couple of cars, and then a red convertible Porsche flew around the turn. There was something about it that made Herb hold his fire. Perhaps it was because the car cost over fifty grand. Certainly he couldn't see who was in it. The Milky Way was glowing above them, but there was no moon. Of course the rest of the gang was in seventh heaven when they saw it was a convertible. They didn't even wait until the Porsche had finished coming out of the turn. All three of them let fly with water balloons. Sammie's and Theo's exploded on the front hood, but it looked like Roger's landed on the driver's face.

The guy behind the wheel lost control only slightly. He swerved off the road but stopped neatly on the shoulder, more than thirty feet from where Roger and Lisa would later take the plunge. A cloud of dust billowed up around the Porsche—the dust mixed with the water must have created a fine mess. The guy was furious. He jumped out of the car along with the passenger, who was a woman with long hair. He started shouting and cursing in their direction, though it was unlikely he could even see them. Roger loved it. He let fly a balloon and hit the guy right in the chest. Then he hit the woman in the head. He and Theo were laughing like maniacs. They thought the two below had had enough because they angrily hopped back in their Porsche and pulled away. But the couple only went a few feet before they opened fire—and their ammunition was a lot more lethal than water balloons.

The first bullet hit a boulder not four feet in front of Herb. If it had continued on its path, it would probably have got him in the groin. The next bullet struck Roger in the right side. It only nicked him, but they didn't know that at the time. All they could see was the blood soaking through his shirt. It was funny about blood—even in the blackness of a moonless night, it was clearly visible. The four of them threw themselves to the ground and trembled while four more bullets whizzed harmlessly over their heads.

Then the couple in the Porsche laughed and drove off.

Roger had to go to the doctor for stitches. He was treated by the same doctor who would sign his death certificate a year later.

They didn't play water balloons anymore. They drank their beer in the park.

But I looked for a water balloon around Roger's burnt car. There wasn't one. There wasn't even any water. There was nothing, except dry ashes. Ashes and cocaine.

Alexa was standing out in front of her house when Herb pulled up. He was happy to see no sign of Lisa's blue Celica. Alexa didn't even let him turn off his engine. She ran around to the passenger side and jumped in.

"What took you so long?" she asked.

"I got lost."

"What?"

"I got attacked," Herb said.

"What?"

"Stephen jumped me down on the strip. He took the picture."

"You're kidding," Alexa said.

"I'm not."

'How did Stephen know you were coming to my house with the picture?"

"I don't know."

"Did you tell anyone you were coming?"

"No," Herb said.

"Did Sammie come to your house?"

"Yeah."

"Did she overhear us talking on the phone?" Alexa asked.

"I don't think so. She had already left." Yet Herb wondered if it was necessary for Sammie to have heard. She was convinced he had the photos, and that he had been talking to Alexa. Sammie could easily have deduced that he would take the pictures to Alexa. But then what? Sammie couldn't have called Stephen and told him to hijack Herb Trasker. Sammie didn't even know Stephen, not as far as Herb knew.

126

"Sammie must have known you had those pictures," Alexa said. "Is that possible?"

Herb shrugged. "I suppose."

"How did you get away from Stephen?"

"Theo came to my rescue," he admitted sheepishly.

"Theo? What could he do against Stephen?"

"He had a gun with him."

Alexa was aghast. "He threatened Stephen with a gun?"

"He shot at Stephen. He didn't hit him, though. He's kind of drunk. God, I hope Stephen doesn't kill him tomorrow."

"Stephen is more talk than anything. Who do you think shot the pictures? Sammie?"

"I doubt it. Sammie couldn't take a picture of a statue in broad daylight."

Alexa was watching him intently. "Then who took them, Herb? Who?"

"Do you think it was me?"

"No. But I wonder why whoever took them wanted you to develop them."

"It does seem strange."

"Are you sure you made only one copy of the picture?"

"Yeah. One eight-by-eleven."

"An eight-by-eleven? Why did you make it so big?"

"That's not big," Herb said defensively. "I could have made it poster size if I'd wanted."

"What about the negative? Did Stephen steal that, too?"

"No. I've still got it."

"Give it to me," Alexa said.

"I didn't bring it with me."

"Why not?"

"You didn't tell me to bring it."

"Where is it?"

"At home, in my bedroom."

"Your bedroom?" Alexa asked, annoyed. "Sammie could just walk in and take it out of your bedroom."

"Why would she do that?"

"Why was she knocking on your door in the middle of the night?"

"I don't know," Herb said vaguely.

"I know damn well what she was doing. She's the one who gave me a ride home from the police station, remember? She thinks I murdered Lisa."

"Did she tell you that?"

"Did she tell you?" Alexa shot back.

Herb shrugged again. "Sort of."

"Sort of? How can someone sort of accuse someone of murder? Did she say it or not?"

Herb spoke carefully. "She thought maybe you had done it."

"And she wanted to see the pictures to be sure, right?"

"I didn't say Sammie asked about the pictures."

"Herb, get off it. Of course she knows about the pictures. She must have taken them. She probably

gave them to you to involve you in some way."
Alexa sat for a moment, drumming her fingers on
the dashboard. "We've got to get that negative
before Sammie does."

"Don't you want to call Stephen and ask him
about the picture he stole from me?"

"Yeah. But let me call him from your house. The
first priority is to stop Sammie."

"Do you think she murdered Lisa?" Herb asked.

"I don't think Lisa was murdered. I think her
coke habit simply caught up with her. But I do
think Sammie is trying to use Lisa's accident to get
me in trouble."

"Why?"

"I don't know," Alexa said. "I hardly know
Sammie. Maybe you can tell me why. But do it
while we're driving. Let's go!"

Herb drove back to his house as fast as his
Mustang would allow. He didn't offer Alexa any
theories as to why Sammie was plotting to put her
in jail. He had never known Sammie to do anything
hurtful, except bad-mouth the cheerleaders.

Herb was relieved to see that no one was waiting
outside his house. He had half expected to find
Sammie, Theo, and Stephen all at war on his front
lawn. He felt self-conscious as he parked and
walked up to the front door with Alexa by his
side. His house was small compared to Alexa's,
and he hated Alexa to know just how broke they
were.

His mom was waiting up in the living room,

reading a *Time* magazine. She stood and pulled her robe together when she saw Alexa. She smiled. Alexa smiled also and quickly offered her hand.

"Mrs. Trasker, I'm pleased to meet you," Alexa said. "I'm Alexa Close. I'm sorry it's the middle of the night. I hope I have nothing to do with your being up so late."

Mrs. Trasker shook Alexa's hand. "No, I often go to bed in the early morning hours. Herb and I both do. It's a bad habit we share. I'm pleased to meet you, Alexa, and I was sorry to hear what happened to your friend."

Alexa's smile faltered, though she tried bravely to maintain it. "Lisa was always a terrible driver," she said.

Herb's mother gave her a sympathetic look. "I'm sure you miss her a lot already."

Alexa nodded. "I do."

Mrs. Trasker glanced at Herb. "I suppose I should be off to bed," she said. "There's food in the icebox, if either of you is hungry."

"I'll be taking Alexa home in a few minutes," Herb said. "We're just here to pick up some photographs."

His mother turned toward her bedroom. She was happy he had a girl with him, Herb could tell, even a grieving one. She often told him he should be dating. Of course, she had never told him where to find a date.

"Have Alexa stay as long as she likes," his mother said.

"Good night, Mom."

"Thanks, Mrs. Trasker," Alexa called.

"Good night, Herb. You take care, Alexa." His mother stopped just before she entered her room. "Oh, Sammie called."

"What did she want?" Herb asked.

"She didn't say. I told her you were out. She said she'd call back."

"OK," Herb said.

"I'll see you both later," his mother said. She disappeared through a door at the end of the short hall.

"She's a nice woman," Alexa said, staring after her. "She's not like my mom at all."

Herb chuckled. "The way you say that, you make it sound as if your mom beat you."

Alexa smiled thinly. "No, it's my dad who beat me." She added softly, "And other things."

Herb froze. "What other things?"

"The kind of things you read about in women's magazines. The kind of things TV preachers talk about as signs of the coming of the Antichrist. Those kind of other things."

Herb felt tongue-tied. "You mean sexual abuse?"

"Yeah." Alexa turned her head toward him, and the light in her green eyes was cold. "But let's just say that my dad hasn't bothered me in a while. I gave him something that he'll remember for a long time."

"I'm real sorry to hear about this. I don't know what to say."

Alexa shrugged. "Don't worry about it. I don't."

"Could I get you something to eat or drink?" Herb paused. "What am I saying? You want to know if the negative is still here. Let me check."

Alexa stopped him, touching his arm. "It's got to be here. Your mom was waiting up, and Sammie just called, so she didn't come back here."

Herb nodded. "You're right."

Alexa moved around the room, checking out the paintings on the wall, the furniture. Herb's uneasiness over their limited economic situation intensified. "You know what I'd like?" she said. "A sandwich. I haven't eaten all day."

"Sure. What would you like on it?"

"Everything you've got. Do you guys drink beer?"

"Yeah."

"I'd like a couple of beers, too," Alexa said. "I like them ice-cold."

"Coming right up," Herb said.

Fifteen minutes later they were sitting in the kitchen eating. Alexa's appetite was enormous. Herb had taken beef, ham, and turkey cold cuts from the refrigerator, and she had told him to pile them all on, adding lettuce and tomatoes herself. She drank her beers iced from a single thirty-two-ounce glass. The ice cracked together every time she raised the glass to her lush lips. She looked very sexy as she chewed with a full mouth, and Herb found himself marveling over the fact that she was sitting with him in the middle of the night, when she could probably have been with anyone else in the world. She had on the same white pants she had worn to the police station, but her blouse was now black, thin and silky. It was obvious she wore no bra underneath.

"Aren't you hungry?" Alexa asked, reaching for an open bag of potato chips. Herb had made himself a smaller version of Alexa's sandwich, but he didn't care for it. Ordinarily he never mixed different kinds of meats. He had read somewhere that it was bad for the heart.

"Yeah," Herb said, taking a bite of his sandwich.

"That's good," she mumbled as she took a slug of beer. She set down her glass and wiped her lips with the back of her hand. "So here we are, stuffing our faces with cold cuts while Lisa is lying cold in a morgue somewhere."

"You're not still blaming yourself, are you?"

"Sure I am. I knew Lisa took coke. I never tried to stop her from taking it. Doesn't that make me partly responsible?"

"No," Herb said. "You can't stop someone from taking drugs if they don't want to stop."

"Who told you that?"

"I read it in a magazine."

Alexa put a handful of chips in her mouth. "That's B.S. This is Mannville, it ain't L.A. I could have cut off her supply."

"How?"

"I'm Stephen's girlfriend."

"Stephen sold her the drugs?"

"Stephen *got* her the drugs. Sometimes he sold them to her. Sometimes he gave them to her." Alexa added, "I told you he was a creep."

"Then why do you go out with him?"

Alexa sat back and stared at her sandwich. "He knows how to cook."

"Huh?"

"Nothing, that was just a joke." She smiled suddenly, her long hair framing her soft face. "Tell me about yourself."

"There's nothing to tell."

"Come on. How did you get into photography?"

"My mom gave me a camera when I was a kid. I just started taking pictures. I liked how different things looked in pictures."

"How do they look different?"

Herb thought a moment. "They're even more real."

"That's interesting. Do I look more real in pictures?" Alexa set her sandwich down and leaned closer. "More real than I look now?"

Herb was embarrassed. "You always look just fine to me."

Alexa liked that. "You always look just fine to me, too, Herb, and I haven't even seen a picture of you." She stood up suddenly. "Let me see your darkroom."

"It's in my bedroom."

She spoke in a naughty tone. "Don't you let girls go in your bedroom?"

It was a sad fact, but he had never had a girl who

wanted to go into his bedroom, except Sammie, who didn't really count. "Sure." He climbed awkwardly to his feet. "We'll have to be careful we don't wake my mom."

"I'm not that loud, Herb," she said with a straight face.

His room was a mess. It always was. His bed wasn't even made. He felt more embarrassed. Fortunately, he was a couple of seconds ahead of Alexa. He was able to grab a towel and throw it over his camera-VCR fusion. Alexa entered at his back and scanned the room closely, but not critically. She stepped inside and sat on the edge of his bed. She nodded to the work area in the corner, the vinyl sheets that half hid his darkroom.

"Is that where you make your prints?" she asked.

"Yeah."

"Make one for me from the negative you have of Lisa and me in the showers."

Herb felt the blood rise to the surface in his face. "You weren't exactly in the shower."

"I understand. But I want to see the picture."

"You could just look at the negative with my loupe—it's a small magnifier. Another print will take a while to make."

"How long?"

"Ten minutes."

Alexa checked her watch. "That isn't long. I can't tell anything from a negative."

"OK."

The negative was where he had left it. Herb

repeated the procedure he had performed earlier, starting from the point where he had a workable negative. He inserted the negative into the negative holder, placing it inside the enlarger, turning on the safelight, turning off the ordinary light, and focusing the enlarger on the easel that held the photographic paper. He explained as he went along, and Alexa asked a number of questions. She appeared genuinely interested in the art of producing a picture. And it was an art, he told her. He had spent many years becoming as good as he was.

Alexa stood by his side when he had the safelight on. In the softness of the red glow she appeared particularly seductive. She stood *very* close to his side. He could hear her breathing and feel the warmth from her skin near his exposed flesh. He imagined he could even hear her heartbeat as he slipped the paper into the Dektol and gently stirred it around. It was at this point that the image of Alexa approaching Lisa with the baseball bat was made clear to Alexa for the first time.

"When was this picture taken?" Alexa whispered, her eyes glued to the print as it lay beneath an inch of solution. Her vision stayed focused that way for several seconds, then she raised her head suddenly and stared far off for several more seconds. Her demeanor changed completely in that time. It was as if something crucial had just struck her. A thrill of excitement shot through her features, but she appeared to strain to keep it under control.

"This afternoon," Herb said.

Alexa slowly tilted her head his way. "How do you know it was taken this afternoon?" she asked softly.

Herb felt flustered. "That's what the note said."

"Could I see this note?"

"I don't know where I put it."

"Would you like to see my note?" Alexa asked.

"Sure, I guess. But what for?"

She brought out a piece of folded white paper and handed it to him. It wasn't much of a revelation, not now. In the center, typed in neat capital letters, was the sentence Alexa had already described.

WE HAVE PICTURES OF WHAT YOU DID
TO LISA.

"It says *we*," Alexa said.

"Yeah."

"Who do you think *we* could be, Herb?"

She's asked me that a few times already. She knows I'm lying. Any fool would know I'm lying. I keep sticking my foot in my mouth.

"I don't know," Herb said.

"Well, what do you think of the picture then?"

Herb glanced at the print in the Dektol. He would have to take it out in a second. "It's pretty sharp. It was taken by a good quality camera."

"No," she said. Then she broke into a grin and shook her head. She spoke with peculiar confidence for someone who had been caught in the act. "Herb, I'm carrying a goddamn baseball bat. What does that make you think?"

"That you killed Lisa." He added hastily, "But I don't think that."

"Why not?"

"Because Lisa was your best friend."

She nodded, still watching him, and dropped her grin. "Would you believe me if I told you that picture wasn't taken twelve hours ago, but two weeks ago?"

"Sure," he said, and the lies kept piling up inside his mouth. Yet Alexa surprised him with what she said next. She began to pace his small bedroom in the gloom of the safe light and the smell of vinegar.

"Two weeks ago the squad cheered at a school baseball game," she said. "You may not know this, but we seldom go to the baseball games. We have a lousy team—we always lose. Plus cheerleaders are a waste of time at baseball games. No one cheers, even when their team is winning. Anyway, after the game—it was a home game—Lisa and I helped carry some of the equipment back to the guys' showers. Lisa and I were making fun of the guys. We told them we were going to keep their baseballs and their bats in the girls' equipment cage, and not give them back, because they played so lousy. Lisa and I ran off with the bats and the balls, and they chased us all the way to the girls' showers, but then they had to give up."

"So that's how you happened to have the bat

with you?" Herb asked, feeling relieved. Despite the evidence to the contrary, he had never really believed Alexa had done anything wrong.

Yet his relief was slightly premature. He was forgetting the small fact that his equipment had taken the picture only twelve hours earlier. He had to stop forgetting small details like that.

Alexa stopped her pacing. "Yes, exactly. In fact, I remember walking over to Lisa with a bat in my hand while she was in the shower."

"But who took the picture?" Herb asked.

"Excellent question." Alexa leaned against the board at the end of his bed, which was on the verge of collapsing. "There was someone else with us in the showers that afternoon."

"Sammie?"

"Yes. She was at the game taking pictures for the school annual."

"Are you sure?" Sammie had never mentioned the assignment to him.

"I'm positive," Alexa said, letting her excitement show. "Sammie was in the showers when I was goofing off with Lisa." Alexa pointed to the tray of Dektol. "Don't you have to take the print out?"

It had slipped his mind. Another small detail down the drain. He turned and pulled out the photograph—another eight-by-eleven. He set it on the pile of paper towels he had used earlier and blotted off the moisture. Alexa returned to his side.

"She sure caught Lisa's butt in that one," Alexa said.

"Lisa had a nice butt," Herb muttered, before realizing what he was saying. He flushed with embarrassment, for about the tenth time. "I'm sorry. I didn't mean—"

"It's all right." Alexa nodded to the picture. "Look closely in the upper right-hand corner, in the mirror in front of the equipment cage. Do you see a reflection there?"

Herb leaned over and peered closely. It was seldom that he missed anything in a photo, but earlier his attention had been monopolized by Alexa and Lisa. Now he saw it, though. The reflection in the mirror was faint, blurred. It was a person, yes, but who he or she was was difficult to tell.

"I see her," he muttered. "Or him."

"What is she wearing?" Alexa asked.

"It looks like a plaid shirt."

"What color is her hair?"

"Brown, but in a black-and-white print, it's hard to tell."

"Would you say this girl is on the heavy side?"

"If it is a girl, yeah."

"Of course it's a girl. It's Sammie. She wears plaid shirts."

Herb looked up. "Lots of girls do."

"But few girls have a body like Sammie's. I don't mean to sound crude, but this girl's fat. Sammie's fat. Sammie's got brown hair, cut short. So does this girl. It makes sense. Sammie was there that day two weeks ago. She must be the one who took the pictures."

Herb wanted to agree with Alexa. It would have made it easier to escape from the tangled web he had created with his miserable lying. Yet Sammie was his friend. She had been his friend a lot longer than Alexa had. As far as he knew, Sammie had no reason to set Alexa up for Lisa's murder. Plus, he reminded himself, he had taken the pictures.

"If Sammie took this picture, how can she be in it?" he asked.

"You're the photographer, you tell me."

"She would have to have had an extremely long camera cable. From the angle of this picture, I'd have to say it was taken from—" He had to pause to clear his throat. He knew the angle well. "From high in the corner of the showers."

"Then she must have had a long cable and snapped the picture the moment it looked incriminating for me. Herb, that *is* her in the picture. Study it closely."

He studied the print a bit longer, and perhaps it was his imagination, but the blurred reflection in the mirror did begin to resemble Sammie. Indeed, the girl in the photo had what could have been the worst haircut in the world, another Sammie Smith trademark. He sat back, thinking. It was then an extraordinary idea flattened his logical processes.

What if the film I removed from the camera was not the same film I put in? What if these pictures really were taken two weeks ago? What if Alexa is right, even if it is for all the wrong reasons?

What if Sammie really had taken the pictures?

It made sense, in a way. The idea of the pictures had been Sammie's. Just as important, the timetable of when the pictures were to be taken had been Sammie's. She had even designated the spot where he should place his camera. Why? Because she had taken pictures from the same location? Because she wanted hers to match his? Because she wanted him to think hers had been his?

If the timing was important to Sammie, that meant . . .

Sammie had known Lisa was going to die Friday afternoon.

When did someone know exactly when someone else was going to die?

Answer—when he or she was going to be the murderer.

Herb felt sick. He went over to his bed and sat down. Alexa sat beside him. She put a hand on his shoulder.

"It is true, isn't it?" she asked.

He nodded weakly. "It might be. But Sammie was with us from the time Lisa died. How did she put the note in your room?"

"She could have done it before Lisa died. If she knew Lisa was going to be dead by the time I read it."

"But you've been saying all along that Lisa wasn't murdered."

"I'm beginning to change my mind."

Herb shook his head. "But I've known Sammie since I was a kid. She's never hurt anybody."

"I know how you must feel," Alexa said gently. "No, I take that back. I can't know how you feel. But you have to understand how *I* feel. My best friend's died mysteriously. There are pictures floating around town that show me preparing to murder her. I'm not going to let myself be set up. I'm sorry, Herb."

He nodded grimly. "I guess you want to go to the police."

"No, not yet. I want to hear Sammie's side of the story first. That's only fair, I think."

"Should we call her?"

Alexa checked her watch. "I'm surprised she hasn't called you back yet."

"You want to wait until she calls?"

"That would be OK," Alexa said.

"Do you want to call Stephen?"

"Yeah, I do." Alexa removed her hand from his shoulder and inched a little closer. "But not right away."

"Aren't you worried about the other print he's got?"

"Nothing about Stephen worries me. He's nothing." Alexa's right thigh was now pressed against his left leg. "He's like my dad in a lot of ways."

"Are you thinking of breaking up with him?"

Alexa touched his hair with the tips of her fingers. "I don't have to think about it. I'll just do it."

"When?"

"Maybe tonight, after I get the picture back from

him." She continued to play with his hair. "What kind of shampoo do you use?"

"Ivory."

"Ivory soap?"

"Yeah, just the bar, you know." He enjoyed her flirting with him—he assumed it was flirting, but he couldn't be sure. He'd only read about the subject in magazines. He did know he was sweating and he was worried about his deodorant wearing off. Alexa had a soft touch. She also smelled nice, like roses.

"Plain soap wrecks your hair, don't you know that?" she said. "Doesn't your mom buy shampoo?"

"She does, but I don't use it." He didn't want it running out on his mom. He chuckled uneasily. "I don't worry too much about the way I look. Can't you tell?"

She smiled, easy and wide, and leaned her head close to his ear. He could feel her breath again, and it was warm and moist. "I think you're cute, Herb." She let her right arm drift across his shoulders. He couldn't believe it—she was actually hanging on to him. "Do you think I'm cute?" she asked.

"I think you're cute, Herb."

"No," he said.

She frowned. "What?"

Did I say no? God, I did. I called her a dog. Lord.

"Yeah, you're the prettiest girl in the school now that Lisa's dead," Herb said enthusiastically.

"Wait. No—what I mean is, you were pretty before she was dead. But now you're prettier."

Alexa laughed softly. "Do I make you nervous?"

He shrugged, but he had trouble stopping shrugging. He looked like he had a bad case of the shakes. "I never get nervous," he said.

Alexa laughed softly and nodded in the direction of his makeshift darkroom. "Lisa does look awfully nasty in that photograph."

There was no sense lying about that one. "Yeah."

She poked him in the side. "Too bad it wasn't me, huh?"

Herb's heart did a nice big flip-flop. Naturally he made another stupid comment. He was really on a roll. "I don't know. I didn't take the pictures."

"Well, if you're nice to me," Alexa said, "maybe I'll let you take a picture of me like that someday."

What did she say? No, she couldn't have said that. I didn't hear that.

"All right," he said without a shred of excitement, but only because he was in shock. Alexa didn't appear to be put off. She ran the fingernails of her right hand through the hair at the back of his head again. It felt great, wonderful, stupendous— even though she did scratch him in the process.

"One of us is going to have to make a move," she said.

He honestly didn't get the hint. He thought maybe she wasn't comfortable the way she was seated. "Would you like to go back in the living room?" he asked.

She laughed, this time out loud. "You are a picture, Herb. Did anyone ever tell you that? You're a picture of innocence."

"I guess."

Alexa reached over and cupped his face in her hands. She held him tight—her nails scratched him again, this time on his cheeks. She made him look straight into her eyes. They weren't the flawless green he had imagined—numerous black spots floated around her pupils like black holes drifting in a tropical sea.

"You're going to have to kiss me," she said. "You know that."

So Herb kissed her. What was the big deal? He gave her a big, long deep smooch. His heart began to palpitate as their lips touched because he forgot to take in air first. He really had no idea how to do it. He held his breath the whole time they *did it.* Yet even though he was uncomfortable, he liked the feel of her mouth on his. It was like a fantasy. When she pulled away, he felt disappointed, but it was good to take in a fresh lungful of air. He panted like a dog for a few seconds while she sat and smiled at him.

"I'd try to seduce you if we had a heart-lung machine in the room," she said.

He felt a stab of courage. "Don't let that stop you."

She brought her face close to his again. The way she swooped in, and swooped back, it was as if she had wings and could fly. They were flying together

146

in his head. Herb felt a soft warm glow emanating from his chest. He wondered if he was falling in love.

"What are you thinking?" she asked.

"About eagles," he said.

"Tell me."

"You remind me of an eagle."

Her nails plunged once more through his shaggy hair. "How?" she asked. "Am I an endangered species?"

"Yeah." She had made it easy for him to respond. And besides, what she said was true. There weren't too many girls like Alexa around. She nuzzled her cheek against his.

"I've always thought of myself as more of a hawk," she whispered.

"Why?"

"I can't tell you. It's a secret." She sat back slightly, and began to fiddle with the buttons of his shirt. Actually, she began to undo them. She had trouble with the second one. So she just snapped it off, and moved on to the third.

"Do you know why I'm doing this?" she asked.

"No." Truer words had never been spoken.

"Because you don't expect me to." Button number three popped open. "Because you're a gentleman. Because I want to, and I can."

"Oh."

She pulled the remainder of the buttons loose with one hard tug, and button number six ended up with number two—on the floor. He hoped his mother could sew them back on later. He was wearing his best shirt. It was the only one he had that was less than a year old.

"What would you say if I told you I wanted to tie you up, Herb?" Alexa asked out of the blue.

Herb fidgeted uneasily, but he was intrigued. "Can I keep my clothes on?"

"Some of them," she said. "Your socks."

God, she's serious. We're going to have sex. Herb Trasker is going to do it with Alexa Close.

But why did she have to tie him up? He hadn't read about that sort of thing in his mother's magazines, although there might have been something about it in *Playboy*. He really should have done his homework better. He didn't suppose there was a chance he could call Theo before they actually did it.

"Can I tie you up, too?" he asked.

"No."

"Why not?"

"Because I'm the girl and you're the boy. Boys are a lot stronger than girls. The only way to make it fair is to tie the boy up. I used to tie Roger up all the time. You know how strong he was."

"Theo's brother?"

"Yeah. He was hard to hold down."

"But wasn't he Lisa's boyfriend?"

Alexa burst out laughing. "Herb, I'm just kidding you. I'm not going to tie you up. I'm not a sicko. My dad's the sicko. Did you really think I was serious?"

"No, but I don't know you very well, you know."

He felt somewhat disappointed. "I can't tell when you're joking."

She saw she might have hurt his feelings. "I wasn't joking when I kissed you, Herb. I'll tell you the real reason I did that. You're a nice guy."

"You told me that earlier."

"Well, I meant it then. You don't try to use people. I know you didn't take those pictures. You have too much class for that."

He managed to keep his face from twitching. "Thank you."

"You're welcome." She giggled. "I was only kidding about the picture, too. But I'll tell you what. If a big movie studio insists I have to do a nude scene in a major motion picture, I'll insist you be behind the camera. I'll have it put in the contract. Is that a deal?"

He wasn't merely blushing. The better part of his body's blood supply was churning in his cheeks. "Sounds all right by me."

"Good," Alexa said. "Now kiss me again."

Herb didn't get another kiss.

The phone beside his bed rang.

Alexa sat back. "It's probably Sammie. Don't tell her I'm here. She'll want to meet you. Tell her you will, but it has to be at the cliff where Lisa ran off the road."

The phone rang again. It was going to wake his mother.

"Why?" Herb asked.

"Just do it. I'll explain later."

149

Herb picked up the phone. "Hello?" he said.

"Are you all right, buddy?"

Herb covered the phone and spoke to Alexa. "It's Theo."

"Theo's still awake," Alexa muttered to herself thoughtfully.

"I'm fine," Herb told his old friend. "Has Stephen come looking for you yet?"

"If he does, he's going to regret it. Is Sammie there?"

"No. Why?"

"She's looking for you. She just called me."

"Why isn't anyone going to bed tonight?" Herb asked.

"There's something in the air." Theo didn't sound intoxicated any longer. "Are you sure you're alone?"

"Yeah. Why?"

"Just wondering. Sammie said you had some photographs she needed."

"I don't know what she's talking about."

"She says Alexa Close murdered Lisa," Theo said.

"Theo, that's ridiculous."

"Sammie sounds sure about it. But don't get me wrong. If Alexa killed that bitch, I'll be the first one to volunteer at her trial as a character witness."

"I think Sammie's the last person who should be accusing people."

"What did Sammie do wrong?" Theo asked.

"Never mind."

"You know what I think, Herb?"

"What?"

"I think it was karma."

"Who?"

"You know what karma is. That's when you do something to somebody and it comes back to you. Hey, did you have a chance to ask Alexa if she knew where my brother was the day he died?"

"No, I didn't. I'll ask her tomorrow if I see her."

"I guess you think I'm being coldhearted about this whole Lisa thing."

"I do," Herb said. "She was only eighteen."

Theo didn't respond for several seconds. When he did speak, all he said was "You get some sleep, buddy."

"You, too. Bye." Herb set the phone down and turned to Alexa. "I guess you heard what he said."

Alexa wore a blank stare. She shook her head. "I didn't. I was thinking."

"Sammie's telling everybody you murdered Lisa."

Alexa was pissed. "That's just great. Some friends you have. I'm tempted to go straight to the police before we talk to her."

"Why don't you?"

Alexa shook her head. "I'm afraid of making a fool of myself. It's still possible Sammie is just trying to blackmail me, that she didn't do anything to Lisa."

The phone rang again.

"It's probably Sammie," Herb said.

"Remember what I said. Also, if she refuses to come to the cliff, tell her she's in the photograph."

The phone rang once more.

"But I already told her I don't have any photographs," Herb said.

"She knows you do," Alexa said. "She gave them to you."

"Oh." Herb picked up the phone. "Hello?"

"Herb, it's Sammie. Are you alone?"

It was a popular question. "My mom's in the next room sleeping. Theo just called. He says you can't sleep."

"Quit making fun of me. This is serious. I've got to talk to you. I've got to see those photos you took."

Herb's suspicions returned sharply, and he didn't like the feel of them. Alexa sat across from him on the bed, fixing her hair while watching him. She nodded her head gravely.

"How do you know I have any photographs?" he asked.

"Because you're a lousy liar."

"I don't know about that."

"Why are you protecting Alexa?" Sammie demanded. "I'm your friend. What has she ever done for you?"

"I'm not protecting anybody. I'm just trying to figure out what happened to Lisa."

Sammie was a long time answering. "So am I," she said finally.

Herb sighed. "It's three forty-five in the morning. Can't this wait?"

"No. I'm coming back over. Just wait up for me."

"No. If you want to see me, you'll have to meet me at the cliff where Lisa went off the road." Alexa was signaling him. She flashed all her fingers three times. "In thirty fingers," Herb added.

"What?"

"In half an hour."

"Why do you want to meet there for godsakes?" Sammie asked.

Herb shrugged, but the gesture was wasted on Sammie. "It's as good a place as any."

"No, I don't like this. I think you've been talking to Alexa. Is she going to be there?"

"I don't think so."

"You don't think so? What kind of answer is that?"

"She won't be there. Why would she be there?"

"I'm not going to that stupid cliff."

"Fine, then I'll talk to you tomorrow," Herb said.

Sammie chewed on that one for a bit. "If I do go to the cliff, will you let me see the pictures?"

"I guess."

"Then you do have them!"

"Shh." Herb held the phone away from his ear. "You're going to wake my mom."

"What do they show?" Sammie asked. "Do they show Alexa killing Lisa?"

How does she know that? She must have set the whole thing up.

"You'll see soon enough," Herb replied, and now he felt sad. "Give us thirty minutes."

"Who's *us?*" Sammie demanded.

"I mean, me. Give me half an hour."

"You'll definitely bring the pictures?"

"Yeah. You'll see them."

"All right," Sammie said. "Talk to you soon."

"Goodbye." Herb set the phone down and studied Alexa. "We can get to the cliff in less than ten minutes."

Alexa stood from the bed. "I want to go home first."

"Why?"

"I want to get my father's gun."

"What? No. We don't need a gun. It's just Sammie we're going to meet."

Alexa spoke firmly. "Your Sammie may have murdered Lisa. Your Sammie is definitely trying to set me up for Lisa's murder. It's the middle of the night, we're going to meet her in an isolated place, and she's dangerous. I want a gun. My father has a thirty-eight."

"And he's just going to lend it to you?"

"I keep it in my bedroom."

"Really? Why?"

"I thought I made that clear." Alexa straightened her blouse. "I don't like to be bothered in the middle of the night."

These cheerleaders are a lot different than I thought.

"We'll pass Sammie on the road on the way there," Herb said.

"We can take the back road off Tree Lane. It's dusty and dumpy, but it'll get us to my place. Then we can drive to the cliff from the other direction."

"Won't she think that's strange?"

"She won't know. You'll see."

"Should we bring the picture?" Herb asked.

"No. God knows how Sammie will try to use it. Here, give it to me. Give me the negative, too."

Herb got up and did as he was told. Alexa folded the print and slipped it in her back pocket, along with the negative.

"What are we going to talk to Sammie about?" Herb asked.

"The truth. What really happened. What else?"

"She won't like it that you're with me."

"She doesn't have to like it," Alexa said. "Let's go."

They were stepping out the front door when Alexa suddenly stopped.

"What's the matter?" Herb asked.

Alexa flashed a quick smile. "I shouldn't have had that second beer. Just a sec, let me run to the bathroom."

Herb stood in the doorway while Alexa hurried down the hall to the small cubicle across from his mother's bedroom. He watched Alexa turn on the light and shut the door. He heard the water running. She was inside awhile. When she reappeared, her eyes were clear, her face confident. He held the door open for her.

"This is like some kind of bad dream," Herb muttered.

"Dreams are never this bad," she said. "You always wake up, sooner or later."

CHAPTER ELEVEN

Herb had lived in Mannville all his life but had never taken the back road Alexa mentioned. He didn't plan to use it again—it wasn't simply bumpy, it was perilous. His Mustang's front bumper got jarred loose before they were halfway to Alexa's house.

"You drive this a lot?" he said, wondering if it was possible to get seasick on dry ground.

Alexa was amused. "You should try it on a motorcycle. It's wild."

Alexa instructed him to park in the driveway. She didn't seem to be concerned about waking her parents, but she wanted him to stay in the car while she went in the house.

"I won't be long," she said, getting out. She had the negative and the print with her.

"Do you know what you're doing?" he asked.

That also amused her. "Who does?" she asked.

She was in the house a long time—fifteen minutes, at least—and they would be late meeting Sammie. Herb began to worry. Alexa had dropped nasty hints about her father. What if she had accidentally awakened him while she searched for the gun? What would a jerk like that do in a bad mood? Herb decided to check on Alexa.

The front door was unlocked, slightly ajar. Herb peeked in. The living room was dark, except for the bluish light from a portable TV wedged in a wooden wall unit. The TV was tuned to an old black-and-white film, with the sound off. The sober light spilled across a gray-carpeted floor and cast haunting shadows around the otherwise innocent furniture. Herb stuck his head all the way inside the door. The living room appeared to be empty.

"Alexa?" he called softly.

No answer. He stepped inside. The house was big—compared to his own it was a mansion—yet it felt oddly claustrophobic. He noticed an empty wheelchair near the couch. The shifting character on the TV set sent glitter and gloom over the stainless steel handlebars. Herb didn't know there was an invalid in the house.

"Alexa?" he whispered. He walked into the center of the room before pausing to listen. There was a sound that took him several seconds to identify. It was breathing, ragged and tired. It took him several more seconds to realize it was coming from a man sitting in a chair at the far end of the room.

God, he sounds like he has lung cancer.

The guy was asleep, his lower body covered with a dark red blanket. He looked extremely uncomfortable—his bony head was bent at such an extreme angle on his hunched right shoulder that his neck could have been broken.

A hand touched Herb's shoulder.

"Ahh!" he cried.

"Shh," Alexa scolded in his ear. She had come out a door behind him. She quickly moved beside him.

The man had opened his eyes and was staring vacantly at Herb. His pale flesh hung flaccidly on his face, yet he wasn't an old man, merely, it seemed, beaten. His green eyes blinked at Herb over and over without seeming to register his being there. He tried to straighten his neck, but it appeared the bones had fused in a twisted way.

"I gave him something that he'll remember for a long time."

"It's just a friend of mine," Alexa told the man. "Go back to sleep."

The man stared at Herb a few seconds longer before doing what he was told. Herb imagined he could see the black-and-white character on the TV set flittering in the depths of the man's blank pupils.

Movies might be his only life now.

When the man closed his eyes, he was asleep in a few seconds, his head back on his shoulder. Alexa turned to face Herb. She was holding the revolver in her right hand.

"What are you doing here?" she asked.

"You were taking a long time. I was worried about you."

She touched his cheek with her free hand. "That was sweet."

Herb found he was shivering, even though the room was warm and stuffy. "Where's your mom? Is she awake?"

"She never wakes during the night. She takes enough pills to make sure that never happens—no matter what's going on." Alexa checked her watch and gestured to the door. "Let's get out of here."

They took the usual road out of the heights toward the cliff. But well before the designated meeting spot, Alexa had Herb pull over to the side of the road. When they were sitting on the shoulder, Alexa rolled down her window and cocked her head to one side.

"I hear someone coming," she said.

"It could be anyone coming up the road," Herb said. "Or it could be Sammie."

"Sammie should be at the cliff already. We're forty-five minutes late." Alexa stared down the road. Because of the many turns and twists in the road, it was unlikely she could see anything. She seemed to be thinking. "Turn off the car," she said suddenly. "I want to get out and walk."

"We still have a ways to go," Herb said. "Maybe as much as half a mile."

Alexa opened her door, and Herb caught a glimpse of the revolver sticking out of her belt. Alexa had donned a loose-fitting shirt, presumably to hide the weapon. "I don't care," she said. "I'm beginning to think Sammie's not coming to this meeting alone."

Herb got out quickly. "Who do you think's going to be with her?"

"I don't know. Theo. Stephen."

"Theo's my best friend. He wouldn't be involved in anything bad."

"Your best friend has been driving around in the middle of the night shooting at people," Alexa said as they moved briskly away from the car. "And Stephen's been involved in many bad things. He may be involved in this. I tried to get him on the phone when we were at my house. He wasn't there." Alexa stopped in midstride. "Hear that?"

"I don't hear anything." He hadn't heard anything when they first stopped the car, either.

"That's my point," Alexa said. "The car that was coming up the hill has stopped. I bet it's at the bend just before the cliff. I want to go off the road."

"You want to sneak up on Sammie?"

"It's better than having her sneak up on us," Alexa said.

It was almost five in the morning. Dawn was only an hour and a half away. The moon had finally risen. A dull yellow quarter crescent, it hung above the dark hills like an artist's tired afterthought, shedding little light to guide them. Alexa walked quickly but silently. Herb convinced her to stay on the shoulder of the road, but he kicked small stones and made noise. Twice Alexa stopped to tell him to be quiet. She became tenser the closer they got to the cliff. When they reached the bend in the road a hundred yards before the cliff, Alexa stopped again and pulled the gun from her belt.

"Are you a good shot?" she asked.

"I shoot with Theo sometimes." He knew the accuracy of most handguns. Anyone would be lucky to hit a human target at forty feet.

She handed him the revolver. "Then you take this. I talk tough, but when it comes down to it, I'm a coward."

Herb didn't want the gun, but he stuffed it in his belt. "I don't think we're going to need this."

"I hope you're right," Alexa said. "But keep it. Keep it handy."

They cut a few yards off the road now. The gorge cut steeply down—five feet from the edge of the shoulder and the tops of their heads were level with the road. The nasty sticky shrubs started a few feet below. By staying on a straight path they were able to walk without too much difficulty. But they did have to lean hard into the hill and support themselves with their hands. The hill became more of a straight wall the closer they approached the point where Lisa's car went flying. The soil beneath their feet was soft and had a tendency to give way if they stepped too hard. Herb tried not to look down. He was reminded of the time he walked the ledge in the girls' showers—it seemed like years ago.

They heard Sammie as they came around the bend. They inched up and saw her standing near the edge of the cliff, on their side of the road. Her car was parked across the street, on the opposite shoulder. She paced as she waited. It was clear she was growing anxious. She kept checking her watch. From all appearances, she was alone.

Alexa and Herb halted about fifty yards from her. They leaned forward with their palms resting on the side of the hill, peering above the edge of the road. Actually, Herb had to grip the hill with the tips of his fingers. If he so much as leaned back, he would topple over. He could now see the wreck of Lisa's car—black and silent on the floor of the gorge.

"Now what?" he whispered.

"We wait and see what she does," Alexa said.

"If we wait too long she'll drive away. Let's talk to her and get it over with. She's alone."

"How do you know she doesn't have an accomplice?" Alexa gestured to the hill above the road, to the spot where Roger and the rest of them had stood during the water balloon war. "She could have someone up there."

"Who?" Herb asked.

"I told you, I don't know. Look, I realize I'm being paranoid. But it's possible if we wait long enough, Sammie will call for her partner to come down."

"And if she doesn't?"

"If she starts to leave, then we'll stop her and demand that she explain the photos."

"All right," Herb said.

They didn't have long to wait for something to happen. A blue Celica—*Lisa's* blue Celica—suddenly appeared from the direction of town. It was traveling at high speed, but it ground to a halt in front of Sammie. She jumped at its arrival, and backed up as Stephen climbed out from behind the wheel. He appeared to be alone, not that he was the sort who'd need help. He slammed the car door shut and stalked Sammie.

"What are you doing here?" Sammie called.

"I've come for a package," he said. He stopped twenty feet from her and hooked his thumbs into his pockets as if he were an Old West gunslinger. Herb only saw this in outline because the night hung over his eyes like a smoky curtain.

"What package is that?" Sammie asked, her voice unsteady. She had her back to the cliff. If she stepped backward another ten feet she'd go over the edge. Herb hoped she knew that. He was beginning to worry about her.

"Don't give me that crap," Stephen said angrily.

"I don't know what you're talking about," Sammie said.

"What is he doing here?" Herb whispered to Alexa.

"I left a note on his machine to call me when he came in," Alexa whispered back. "I said it was important. He might have called me after we left. He might have been on his way to my house."

"What's the package?" Herb asked.

Alexa shook her head. "Maybe it was a package of cocaine. Let's listen."

Stephen took a step toward Sammie. He glanced first to his left, then to his right. From his stance, he appeared to be trying to make up his mind about something, perhaps how far he could push Sammie. He took in a deep shuddering breath and sounded like a bull ready to charge. He looked as strung out as when he had attacked Herb.

"I want the package you stole from Lisa," Stephen said to Sammie. "If you don't hand it over right away, you'll be sorry."

"I didn't take anything from Lisa," Sammie snapped back. She was trying to act tough, but Herb could tell she was scared.

Stephen snorted. "You're a liar."

"Don't call me a liar," Sammie said.

"I'll call you what I want," Stephen said. He came three steps closer. The way he moved— approaching and stopping—was as if he were taunting her.

"What are you doing here?" Sammie asked again. "Did Alexa send you?"

Stephen thought that was funny. He laughed out loud, a deep laugh, cruel and miserable. It struck Herb then that Stephen was in pain. He wasn't merely wired—his limbs were twitching now as if he had a case of epilepsy.

"Alexa doesn't know nothing," Stephen told Sammie. "She doesn't even know what you did to Lisa this afternoon."

"I didn't do anything to Lisa," Sammie protested. "It was Alexa who did it."

Stephen was not impressed. "Did what?"

"Killed Lisa," Sammie said.

"How did she kill her?" Stephen asked.

"With a baseball bat," Sammie said. "She killed her in the girls' showers and dragged her up here and put her in your car and dumped her off the cliff."

"How do you know this?" Stephen asked.

"I have pictures. A friend of mine took pictures."

"Who?" Stephen demanded.

"Herb Trasker," Sammie said.

Thank you for mentioning me to him.

Stephen thought about Sammie's comment, as best he could for someone with an apparent ten thousand volts blasting through his nervous system. Herb guessed that what Alexa said about the mysterious package was correct. Stephen had many of the symptoms of someone strung out on coke.

"How did Trasker take these pictures?" Stephen finally asked. "Was he in the showers?"

"It's a long story," Sammie said.

Stephen spoke savagely. "Tell me!"

"He wired his camera to an electronics box," Sammie said. "He hid it in the showers near the windows. He was able to program it to take pictures at just the right time."

166

"What's she talking about?" Alexa whispered.

"I don't know," Herb said.

"The Herb I know couldn't wire his TV set to a wall plug," Stephen said. "You're feeding me a line. How do you know all this?"

"Herb told me," Sammie said.

"Why would he tell you?" Stephen asked.

"I'm his friend," Sammie said.

I don't know if I need friends like this.

"Was Herb up here when Lisa went off the cliff?" Stephen asked. "Did he have a camera and an electronics box sitting in these hills?"

"No," Sammie said. "Just in the showers."

"Then how do you know how Lisa went off the cliff?" Stephen said. "Or did Alexa tell you that? Why is everyone telling you stuff? What's so special about you? I think you're full of it. I think you ran Lisa off the cliff." Stephen raised his voice. "The same way you ran Roger Corbin off the cliff."

Sammie jumped as if she'd been struck. Stephen had hit a nerve. Herb leaned forward, curious— Sammie had always acted weird when the subject of Roger's death was raised. Herb passed it off as simple grief, even though the explanation never completely satisfied him. For example, Sammie hadn't gone to Roger's funeral, even though they'd known each other for years. She had pleaded illness, but Herb had seen her later that same day stuffing her face in McDonald's. Plus Sammie had been so emphatic about telling everyone she met that Lisa had been in Parvo when Roger had died.

Like she was protecting Lisa. Like they were in it together.

"You're mad," Sammie told Stephen.

"Am I?" Stephen chuckled bitterly. "Lisa told me about that day. She told me everything."

"I wasn't even there," Sammie said. "Lisa wasn't there. We were at the movies in Parvo."

"What movie did you see?" Stephen asked.

"I don't r-remember," Sammie stuttered.

"You don't remember because you didn't see anything." Stephen stalked closer. Sammie backed up. "You killed him. You killed Roger."

"No," Sammie said. "I told you, I wasn't there."

"You drove him off the road in your car," Stephen said, still approaching.

"That's not true!"

"You made Lisa help you cover it up."

Again Stephen had pressed a nerve in Sammie. He obviously knew something. A thin squeal escaped Sammie's lips. She could have just been informed she had a fatal disease, although it was another person's death they were discussing. Her shoulders sagged forward and she rocked on her feet as if she would topple over.

"It wasn't my fault," Sammie cried. "It was Lisa's fault."

"Lisa's fault!" Stephen said with scorn. "Lisa's only fault ever was to get mixed up with you. You cut in front of Roger." Stephen gestured angrily to the road behind him. "You sent him spinning out of control."

Sammie wept. "I couldn't help it! It wasn't my fault!"

"You lied to everybody!" Stephen swore at her. "You're lying now!"

"I had to!" Sammie moaned.

Oh, God, she did kill Roger.

Stephen paused—he was now less than six feet from Sammie—and pumped up his biceps. Even in a night of shadow, they were daunting—all sinew and sweat. When he spoke next, it was in a softer tone, but no less threatening.

"I want the package," he said.

"What package?" Sammie pleaded. "I don't know anything about a package."

Stephen's right hand went to his right pocket. He appeared to withdraw something from it, but what it was Herb couldn't tell. "If you don't give it to me right now," Stephen swore, "I'm going to cut out your tongue and make you eat it." He took a huge step closer.

It must be a knife.

Sammie quickly withdrew something from her own right pocket. Herb could see this object.

A gun.

Sammie's got a gun. Alexa's got a gun. Theo's got a gun. All the kids in this town are crazy.

"Don't come any closer," Sammie warned.

"You don't have the guts to shoot me," Stephen said, unafraid.

"I mean it," Sammie said, moving back one step farther. The lip of the cliff was practically kissing the back of her heels. She hadn't glanced over her shoulder in a while. Herb suspected Stephen was going to try to make her take the fatal step herself, without touching her. If that was his plan, he should have picked a girl not so well armed.

I've got to stop her. I've got to stop them both.

Herb felt panicked. His heart was a machine in his chest set on overload. But it was the only part of his body that was moving. He was no hero. His muscles had frozen and cold sweat poured off his face and down his neck. Alexa was shaking him.

"Give me the gun," she hissed.

"No," Herb gasped.

"She's going to shoot him," Alexa said.

Herb shook his head. It was hard for him to speak over the knot in his throat. "We can't use it," he gasped. "Just shout, say something. Stop them."

Stephen sneered. "If you shoot me, you'll go to jail."

Sammie coughed weakly. "Please stop. Don't make me do it."

Stephen laughed. "You do what you want and I'll do what I want. I want to watch you fall—all the way to the bottom where Lisa burned."

Sammie wept openly, yet she held her gun evenly. "I swear I'll shoot you. I'll shoot you dead."

"Go ahead," Stephen said, taking one last step toward her.

Many things happened in the next few seconds. Herb had trouble keeping track of them all. Suddenly he felt as if he were caught in a cyclone and spun around a million times. When he was thrown down again, it felt like another dimension, where people looked the same but acted differently, where blood stained the ground and no one seemed to mind. But before he could walk over the blood, he had to watch it fall.

"Give me the gun!" Alexa ordered in a shrill voice. He wasn't given a chance to react; she stretched over and yanked the revolver from his belt. He couldn't have moved to stop her anyway. His paralysis kept him rigid. But when Alexa suddenly started to jump up on the road, a semblance of life returned to his limbs. The cliff was a battleground of haunted histories, and he realized if Alexa entered it, she might get hurt. She might die. He moved his arm and grabbed her pants leg as she was hoisting herself onto the dusty asphalt. She stumbled backward as his hand fastened onto her leg.

No! Don't fall!

Seeing how he had upset Alexa's precarious balance, Herb let go of her leg and pressed his hand against her butt. He may have saved her from plunging to her death—he wasn't sure. She shook him off and tried hoisting herself up once more.

"Stop!" Sammie was screaming at Stephen.

He didn't stop. He just kept on coming, his right hand cocked threateningly. Sammie shook her gun at him. Stephen was practically in her face. Intent on each other, neither noticed Alexa climbing onto the road with her own gun. Herb wanted to shout.

He thought if he could just yell Sammie's or Stephen's name loud enough, the madness would stop. But he couldn't find his voice.

"Drill me," Stephen said. "I don't give a damn." And with that he swung his right hand—the hand that might have held a knife—directly at Sammie's face.

An orange spark erupted in the black space between Sammie and Stephen. A roar shook the night. She had shot him at point-blank range.

"No!" Alexa screamed.

Stephen's right arm dropped to his side, but he raised his left hand and touched a spot on his chest, presumably where he'd been shot. Herb couldn't see what Stephen was doing exactly, but Herb had the disturbing thought that Stephen was trying to plug up the hole to keep the blood from pouring out. Stephen stared at Sammie for a moment in what appeared to be immense surprise. Then he dropped to his knees, slowly, falling like a tree that had just been felled. He rolled onto his side, his left hand still pressed to his chest.

"Stop!" Alexa cried. She was on her feet on the road, running toward her boyfriend. Sammie suddenly shifted in Alexa's direction, the smoking gun in her hand doing the same. Alexa raised her own gun above her head as she ran. She fired a single shot toward the sky, perhaps to frighten Sammie into surrendering. It was a foolhardy plan. Herb knew how Sammie must feel. She had just been attacked by an insane man. Now she had a screaming shadow running toward her and blowing off bullets. Sammie hardly hesitated. She pointed her gun at Alexa and fired.

Sammie missed, or so it seemed. The shot didn't slow Alexa at all, and Alexa made no move to shoot Sammie. Herb could see that Alexa had lowered her gun to her side. Sammie, also, appeared to be lowering her weapon. For those reasons the next shot caught Herb completely by surprise. It seemed to come out of the sky—out of nowhere. Yet there was no confusion about who it was aimed at.

Sammie jerked involuntarily toward the edge of the cliff. She let out a faint strangled cry before toppling over the edge. Then her cry changed to a heart-wrenching wail that did not grow fainter as she fell, but louder.

Then it stopped with a sickening thud.

All sound stopped, and there was silence. Herb found he could move again, he could speak again. He climbed up onto the road and scanned his immediate surroundings. Alexa was crouched over Stephen, crying, but no one else was visible. Herb half expected to hear another shot, and feel a bullet plunge into his heart. He felt as if someone had taken a knife and driven it deep into his chest. Two people had just been shot, and one of them was his friend.

Poor Sammie.

Herb staggered toward Alexa. She had Stephen's head cradled in her lap. His blood was all over her and on the ground. It had formed a dark puddle that looked like a hole into hell. Stephen had been shot in the center of the chest, probably directly through the heart. His mouth hung open but he was not breathing. He was dead, Sammie and he both were.

She was alive all the way to the bottom, though. She was alive when she hit.

Herb touched Alexa's shoulder. "We can't stay here," he said urgently. "Whoever fired that shot must still be around." Herb glanced over his head in the direction of the hill above the road. The way the bullet had knocked Sammie backward indicated it had been fired from the hill. Yet he couldn't see anyone up there. Of course, no one knew better than he that there were a hundred boulders to hide behind.

"Oh, God, this can't be," Alexa wept. "He's dead. He's dead." She ran a bloody hand through Stephen's short tan hair and looked up at Herb, her face streaked with tears. "How can he be dead?" she asked.

"Sammie's dead, too," he said, shaking her. "Someone killed her. That someone's around here still. We have to leave!"

Alexa bowed her head against Stephen's chest. "I don't care," she said miserably.

"You have to care! You could be killed."

"You go. Get away. I'll be all right." She continued to stroke the top of Stephen's head. "I deserve to die, anyway."

174

"Don't say that."

"It's true!" she cried, staring up at Herb once more, her bloodstained hair hanging in her face. "I called Stephen. I brought him here. I should have left him alone." She closed her eyes, grimacing. "I was always so mean to him," she moaned. "I always treated him like garbage."

Herb saw that he was not going to be able to budge her, but he had begun to wonder just how real the danger to them was. If the sniper had wanted to kill them, he'd had time and opportunity enough already. They were out in the open, and the way in which the guy had plugged Sammie said he was an excellent shot.

But the bullet didn't kill her. It was the fall, the long fall.

Herb stepped to the edge of the cliff and looked down. It was hard to see—the feeble moonlight didn't reach the depths of the gorge. Nevertheless, he could see where Sammie had fallen. She had not landed on the rocks, but on top of the wreckage of the red Fiat. A charred metal sword pierced straight through her crumpled form.

"We'll meet you there in half an hour."

Herb felt dizzy. He staggered back from the edge, feeling black waves of nausea and guilt roll over him. He was the one who had called Sammie to her death. He didn't yet understand her involvement with Lisa and Roger, but it didn't matter—he and Sammie had grown up together. She was his friend.

He was supposed to protect her, right or wrong. But he couldn't do anything right. He turned his attention back to Alexa.

"Give me your revolver," he said. He didn't see Sammie's gun anywhere. She had probably taken it with her, to the bottom.

Alexa stared at him with uncomprehending eyes. Streaks of Stephen's blood were on her face, and it looked as if she, too, had been shot. "What?" she mumbled.

"I'm going to see who's up on the hill."

She handed over the gun with a limp arm. "Take care."

"Yeah," he said.

Herb didn't hike directly up on the hill, but headed down the road first—maybe six hundred yards. He wanted to try to come at the sniper from behind, and catch him unaware. But it did occur to him that the sniper was probably watching his every move, and knew exactly what he was doing. Nevertheless, he continued on his way. Directly in front of the cliff, the hill was very steep. When the gang had hiked up to their favorite spot, it had always been from the point he was headed to. He didn't stick the revolver back in his belt but kept it ready in his right hand.

A few minutes later he was off the road and climbing through the boulders again. He tried to keep the sound of his breathing low, but it was impossible. He never exercised, and he was in poor shape. His heart was hammering in his chest, and he just hoped it kept beating. It was heavy with grief because he couldn't get the image of Sammie out of his mind, nor could he free himself of the sound of her scream as she fell.

Herb had climbed high into the hill and was directly above Alexa and Stephen when he spotted the bastard with the gun. He was sitting cross-legged on a boulder with his rifle resting on his knees, about a hundred yards below Herb. For a moment Herb considered shooting him in the back. He even raised the revolver and took aim. But he realized it would take a lucky shot to knock the guy out with one try. The guy had a rifle—he could turn and easily kill Herb before Herb could get off a second shot.

I have to get closer.

Herb knelt and removed his shoes. He'd read in a magazine that some thieves went barefoot when they broke into homes. It was quieter. But Herb was outside and he hadn't gone far toward his adversary when he stepped on a sharp pebble and let out a cry.

"Ouch!" he said.

The fellow below slowly turned and glanced back up over his shoulder. "Is that you, Herb?" he called.

It was Theo.

"What are you doing here?" Herb called.

Theo didn't respond. He returned to staring at Alexa and Stephen. Alexa had moved a pace away from her dead boyfriend, but she continued to sit on the ground, and Herb thought he could still hear her crying. Herb hurried down to Theo. Anger burst through his grief.

"You didn't shoot Sammie, did you?" he demanded of Theo, standing by his side. Theo hardly looked up.

"No, it was the other guy," Theo muttered.

Herb glanced around. "Who?" he whispered.

Theo sighed. "Of course it was me. Is there anyone else here with a rifle?"

Herb shook, he was so upset. "How could you kill Sammie? Are you mad?"

Theo cast him a tired eye. "She killed my brother, I killed her. It's as simple as that. If you don't like it, then you can go to hell."

Herb reached down and grabbed Theo's shoulder. "You can go to hell. You never even gave her a chance to explain what happened. You just shot her down in cold blood."

Theo glanced at the hand on his shoulder, but made no move to shake it off. "If I hadn't shot her when I did, would Alexa still be alive?"

Herb let go of him. He let go of the revolver in his hand, and let it drop on the boulder, where it skidded a couple of feet before coming to a halt. "Sammie wouldn't have killed Alexa," he said.

Theo gestured below them. "She killed Stephen. She killed Roger. Why wouldn't she have killed Alexa?"

"That's insane."

Theo spoke sincerely. "She was insane, Herb.

Did you hear the things she said? About you? About Lisa?"

That sobered Herb, but not for the reasons Theo expected.

Everything Sammie said about me was true.

"She's lying dead at the bottom of the gorge," Herb said.

Theo bowed his head. "I know. It was meant to be."

"How did you come to be here?"

"Stephen called me."

"Stephen? Gimme a break."

"He called me about thirty minutes ago," Theo said. "He said he would forgive me shooting at him if I backed him up while he questioned Sammie about my brother's death. He said he knew things about that day that most people didn't know."

"And you believed him?"

"I thought it might be a trap, but he sounded like he knew stuff about Roger." Theo shrugged. "It looks like he did."

Herb stared down at the cliff. Alexa had finally stood. She saw him and waved. Herb waved back, and then he just let his arm fall by his side. He felt suddenly overcome with profound weariness.

"Now what?" he asked.

"We call the police," Theo said. He touched his rifle, running his hand along the barrel. "And I go to jail, and life goes on."

Herb shook his head. "I don't see how it can."

CHAPTER TWELVE

In the End

"So you called us and we came," Fitzsimmons said. "Is that the end of your story?"

"Yeah," Herb said. "What do you think?"

"It's interesting."

"Yeah, I guess it is." Herb sniffed. "It's kind of sad, too, don't you think?"

"That it is, Herb. I'm sorry."

"Now I suppose you'll want to arrest me."

"No, I don't," Fitzsimmons said. "But I do want to ask you a few questions. Let's go back a bit. When you returned for your film after leaving the police station, did you notice any sign that your camera or other equipment had been disturbed?"

"No."

"Were they in the same position as before?"

"As far as I could tell."

"Was the *type* of film you took out of your camera the same as the type you put in?"

"They were both rolls of Kodak, thirty-two exposures," Herb said. "But that's not surprising—everybody in town uses Kodak. It's practically the only film you can buy."

"Are you sure Theo was sound asleep in your living room when you got there?"

"I can't be a hundred percent sure."

"Tell me something, Herb. When you first saw the negative of Alexa sneaking up on Lisa, how come you didn't call us immediately?"

"Because Sammie came over and Theo woke up. Then Alexa called, and everything just started rolling, and it didn't stop until it stopped."

"But that's not the real reason, is it?"

"What do you mean?"

"You wanted to protect Alexa."

Herb hesitated. "I suppose it's possible."

"How did Sammie know you had the picture?"

"I explained that. Because it was hers."

"But let's say it wasn't hers. Let's say Alexa *did* kill Lisa with a baseball bat yesterday afternoon. Sammie could have still known you had the pictures because Sammie suggested the idea to you. She told you where to put your camera. Friday afternoon she could have checked to see if your camera and VCR were in place."

"I follow you," Herb said.

"I just wanted to establish this as a possibility. But if the pictures were taken yesterday afternoon, and not two weeks ago, why did Sammie want you to take them? How did she know they'd reveal a murder? I think those are the central questions we must deal with. Would you agree, Herb?"

"Sure. But I think, no matter which way you look at it, Sammie knew Lisa was going to die. And the only way she could have known that was because she was going to murder her. It doesn't matter when the pictures were taken."

"But it does," Fitzsimmons insisted. "Because if they were taken two weeks ago, we can believe Alexa's explanation of why she was carrying a baseball bat. But if they were taken yesterday, we can't."

"Why not?"

"Because it makes a liar out of Alexa. And once again, it forces us to ask ourselves how Sammie could have known Alexa would be sneaking up on Lisa with a baseball bat at exactly the time your camera was taking pictures. I know I'm repeating myself, but I want to make this point clear."

"I understand," Herb said. "That's why I don't think the pictures were taken yesterday. Otherwise there's no way to explain how Sammie knew."

"But there is a way. It's possible Sammie and Alexa were working together."

Herb almost laughed. "Sammie was doing everything in her power to put Alexa in jail. Sammie even tried to shoot her. I didn't see any signs of cooperation between them."

"That's true," Fitzsimmons said, troubled. "It's a real puzzle."

"Why don't you just believe Alexa's explanation?" Herb asked.

"Because I have no motive why Sammie would go to so much trouble to frame Alexa. What did Alexa ever do to her?"

"Nothing as far as I know," Herb admitted. "They hardly ever talked at school."

"What about Lisa and Sammie?" Fitzsimmons asked.

"I told you. They hardly talked, either."

"Yet Sammie was Lisa's alibi the day Roger died. I find that interesting. You said that Sammie—just before Theo shot her—implied that she was involved with Roger's death. Lisa might also have been involved—and Alexa, too, since she was Lisa's best friend."

"I don't think Alexa was involved."

"Why not?"

"I don't think Alexa had any idea what Sammie was talking about just before Sammie died. You saw Alexa when you arrived last night. She was completely distraught."

"Because of what happened to Stephen," Fitzsimmons said.

"No, because of *all* the deaths. Alexa didn't kill Roger or Lisa or anybody. That should be obvious after what I've told you. Really, Sergeant, how do we know Roger or Lisa were even murdered? There's still no proof that they were, not really."

"That's true," Fitzsimmons said and he sighed again. "But I still have questions. You told Alexa on the phone what the picture revealed. How come she didn't explain what had happened two weeks ago right then?"

"She probably forgot. I don't think the thing with the baseball bat came back to her until she saw the picture with her own eyes."

"But she *wanted* that picture, Herb. She wanted the negative. She didn't want the police to see them. Doesn't that strike you as suspicious?"

"No. If you saw the picture or negative you'd understand. They make her look guilty of something she didn't do. If it had been me in the picture, I wouldn't have shown it to the police."

"But you've told me about it, and I am the police."

Herb stopped. "You said this was all off the record."

"I didn't exactly say that."

Herb sharpened his tone. "Look, you don't have the picture or the negative. You don't have anything."

"Don't get angry."

"Well, I don't think it's fair to Alexa or me to pull stunts like this."

"Is it fair for Lisa's parents and Sammie's and Stephen's to never know the truth?"

"You can tell them what I told you. Just leave out the stuff about my picture. I think that's fair."

"Your picture is everything." Fitzsimmons was quiet for a moment. When he spoke next, it was in a softer, more subdued voice. "Who has the picture and negative now?"

"I assume Alexa still has them."

"Really? I think she's probably destroyed them by now."

"It's possible."

Fitzsimmons appeared to drop the matter. "I talked to Theo this morning. He told me to say hi to you."

"How is he?"

"Confused. Tired. Depressed. He doesn't know how this all got started. His story agrees with yours—the parts he knows."

Herb realized why Fitzsimmons had waited until the end to tell him he had already questioned Theo. Fitzsimmons had wanted to see if they made liars out of each other. Herb understood that it was the sergeant's job, so he wasn't offended. Actually, as they talked, he had grown to like Fitzsimmons. The man was clever, and he did seem to care about the people involved.

"Did Stephen really call Theo and ask him to back him up?" Herb asked.

"That's what Theo says. Doesn't seem likely, from what you've told me about their relationship." Fitzsimmons added, "But I think Theo's telling the truth."

"I don't understand," Herb said.

"I'm not sure I do. Like I said, it's a puzzle. There may have been a murder committed. There may have been more than one. All we know for sure is there are four people dead, and your friend is in jail charged with first degree murder."

"Theo might have saved Alexa's life," Herb said quickly.

"I'm sure the judge and jury will take that into consideration, when and if the case goes to trial." It sounded to Herb as if Fitzsimmons was turning a page in his notepad. "Drugs appear to be an important element here. The complete autopsy isn't in on Stephen, but it's clear he was high on cocaine when he died. There is also evidence of other unusual chemicals in his bloodstream."

"Like what?"

"I don't know. We will have to wait a few hours more until all the test results are complete."

"He acted pretty strung out," Herb said.

"That's what you said. Let's go back to last night. Alexa's excuse for not calling the police after she had seen the photograph—that Sammie had supposedly planted—was that she wanted to hear Sammie's side of the story first. Is that correct?"

"Yeah. I thought Alexa was being very fair about the whole matter."

"But she wanted to hear Sammie only if she had a gun in her hand."

"Alexa only fired her gun once and that was at the sky."

"I believe you," Fitzsimmons said, sounding far from convinced. "Theo says the same thing. That was brave of Alexa—to charge an armed girl who

186

had just shot and killed her boyfriend. Did you know that we've been unable to locate the knife Stephen carried?"

"I never said he had a knife. I *thought* he had one. It was dark. It was hard to tell."

"Did you know Sammie's gun had only two bullets in it?"

"What?" Herb said.

"The gun she used to kill Stephen ordinarily carries six shots. But Sammie loaded it with only a couple of bullets. There were no shells in it when we retrieved it from the gorge."

"Maybe that's all the bullets she had."

"Did you know Sammie owned a gun?"

"No."

"She never talked about it?" Fitzsimmons asked.

"No. Maybe it was her dad's."

"Her father says he's never owned a gun. Where do you think she got it?"

"I have no idea. Can't you check the serial number on it and trace it that way?"

"The serial number had been filed off."

"It's too bad Sammie's not here to tell us about it."

"Where are you coming from, Herb?" Fitzsimmons asked suddenly. "You're protecting Alexa, and by doing so, you're laying all the guilt at Sammie's feet."

The knot in Herb's throat welled up once more, but this time it did not stop at his throat. His eyes moistened, too. "You have no right to say that. I don't want to blame anyone, especially not Sammie. She's not here and can't defend herself." Herb had to take a breath before he could continue. "She was my friend. I would have done anything for her. She would have done anything for me."

"She threatened you at least once during the night."

"She was upset. I wasn't being straight with her and she knew it. Maybe I should have been, and then maybe she'd be alive now."

"What's Alexa to you then?"

Herb coughed. "She's a friend."

"Could she be a girlfriend?"

"Not my girlfriend."

"Why not?"

"She can do better. A lot better."

"Why do you say that? You're not so bad."

"I say it because it's true. Why don't you just close the book on this thing? Let Theo go. He was just trying to protect Alexa."

"Why did Theo have to protect Alexa? Why did Alexa choose that isolated spot to confront Sammie, when she admits she was afraid of Sammie? Why didn't Alexa want to meet Sammie at the Denny's in town? Why did Stephen just happen to drive by? Can you answer these questions, Herb?"

Herb didn't respond, mainly because he didn't know what to say. There was a bird singing outside his window, and he listened to it for a few seconds, hoping the sweet sound would clear his mind. Sammie had had a great singing voice. Sometimes he and Sammie and Theo would be driving around, listening to the radio, and Sammie would begin to sing along with the radio. Most of the time she sounded better than the artist.

But the world won't know what she would have done with that voice. What she would have done with her whole life.

He had told Sammie to go to the cliff. He kept coming back to that.

"Can you answer these questions, Herb?"

Yeah, he could, another voice in his head said. A lot of weird stuff had gone down the last couple of days, but then, the world was a weird place, and that was to be expected. Lisa and Roger were into coke and couldn't drive under the influence. Sammie and Stephen didn't get along, and didn't know how to handle guns and knives. It was all very simple and they were just making it complicated.

But he was carrying a knife. Why can't they find it?

"Alexa said she'd tell you later why she wanted to meet at the cliff," Fitzsimmons said, breaking the long pause.

"Did she?" Herb asked.

"That's what you said."

"I was mistaken."

"She never told you, did she?" Fitzsimmons said.

"No."

"Herb, at the beginning of our conversation you said a friend was coming over to see you."

"I don't remember saying that," Herb lied. It was one of the few things he did remember.

"Is someone coming over?"

"No."

"Is it Alexa?"

"No."

Fitzsimmons stopped his questions for a moment. From the sounds on the phone, Herb decided he was closing his notepad. But his next comment told Herb he wasn't through with the matter—not by a long shot. Fitzsimmons spoke seriously.

"Herb, listen to me," he said. "I asked you this at the beginning and I'm asking you again. Come down to the station now. We need to talk."

"We've been talking all morning. I have nothing else to say."

"But Theo wants to see you. He asked for you."

"Tell him I'll see him later," Herb said.

"When?"

"This afternoon."

"When this afternoon?"

"Two o'clock. I should be ready by then."

Fitzsimmons sighed. "I'm worried, Herb."

"What are you worried about?"

"You."

"I promise I'll be there."

"I'm worried you're not going to make it."

"That's silly," Herb said.

"Can you promise me you won't see Alexa?"

"Why not?"

"I think we both know the answer to that."

Herb swallowed. The lump was back in his throat, the damn lump. He should have it operated on. It might be cancer. It might be something worse.

Like the truth. The truth was supposed to hurt. His throat sure did. His whole body ached.

"Sure, whatever you say," Herb said. "But I'll be fine, really. I'll see you at two. OK?"

Fitzsimmons paused. "What if I come to you?"

"Don't."

"I can be there in about half an hour. I want to come, Herb."

"I don't want you to come."

Fitzsimmons was suddenly in a hurry. "Look, I'll see you soon. Take care."

"You, too," Herb replied, figuring Fitzsimmons would do whatever he wanted no matter what the troubled teenage boy said. Herb put down the phone and listened to his heart beating. It seemed he could hear all his emotions in the beats: grief, weariness, and hope. Yeah, he felt hope. But he didn't know what he was hoping for. There was no hope after death, and in the days to come there would be three funerals to attend.

Or four.

His heart skipped a beat. There was fear there, too, a deep black fear.

Herb stood and went into the bathroom. He

washed his face and brushed his teeth, and pulled on a fresh pair of pants and a clean shirt. He went into the living room. He was surprised that he couldn't find his mother. He had assumed she'd be anxious to hear what the sergeant wanted. Then he saw the note when he went into the kitchen. It was on the table.

> Herb,
>   I'm heading over to Parvo. I need to talk to the authorities myself about what happened last night. Don't be mad at me. I'll call you from there. Stay inside. Stay out of trouble.
>
> Love, Mom

Herb wasn't mad. She was just looking out for him, as mothers the world over did for their children.

"She's a nice woman."

Herb returned to his bedroom and sat on his bed in the exact spot he had after studying the negatives for the first time. He did not, however, continue to think about his mother and what a fine woman she was. He thought about his father, whom he didn't even know, and he grew sad. Maybe if he'd had a strong fatherly figure when he'd been growing up, he wouldn't have turned out to be such a loser, such a pervert. To think he had set up a camera in the girls' showers, believing no harm would come from it. He was a fool on top of everything else. His father had probably known that the moment Herb came out of the womb. No wonder the guy took off.

"But let's just say my dad hasn't bothered me in a while."

Of course, not all fathers were a good influence on their kids. Look at Alexa's father for instance. The guy was obviously sick.

"It's just a friend of mine. Go back to sleep."

The old man had done what Alexa said. After he had stared at Herb for a moment. Herb remembered how the black-and-white characters from the TV had flickered in the depths of the man's eyes. The reruns. The emptiness. How could a grown man, with so much history, have become so empty? What had taken it all away? The cruelty to his daughter? Yes, probably, that and his paralysis, of course.

"I gave him something that he'll remember for a long time."

Herb stood and walked over to his camera that was still hooked to the VCR he had borrowed from work. He lifted up the towel that was hiding them and picked up his camera. His pride and joy. The only thing that separated him from the school's other losers. He opened the back. The camera was empty, of course; the last roll of film he had used had been *the* roll. But that was not a problem. He had plenty of film. Film was cheap. It was subjects that were expensive, particularly if one wanted them pretty and naked. Then all sorts of payments were demanded, including one's own integrity and self-respect. His mouth tasted foul from all the lies he had told in the last two days.

Herb scooped a roll of twenty-four exposures off his desktop and popped it in the back of his camera.

What are you doing? Loading your ammunition? Cameras only fire blanks, you should know that by now.

Herb checked his watch. Ten to twelve. His friend should arrive soon. He plunged the VCR in the electrical outlet and reset the timer. Now he had to make the same decisions all over again. When to start shooting? How far apart to space the shots? Unfortunately, he didn't have Sammie to advise him. Only his own judgment about how fast things could move.

How quickly they could get bad.

"You're going to have to kiss me."

Herb made his decision. He pushed a few buttons on the programming square. Then he recovered the equipment with the towel, leaving the lens free. He aimed it at the bed, focusing on the pillows. Next to his camera, his bed had always been his favorite possession. It was where he dreamed. He remembered the dream Fitzsimmons's call had interrupted. The long hopeless journey through the desert. The crushing thirst. The flies. Roger Corbin riding out of the south like the Grim Reaper. That had been one hell of a nightmare—Roger and his bony hands, and the others, their bleached skeletons under Old West clothes. Lisa, Sammie, Stephen—all corpses, all lost in the wild. Of course, they had been dead before his dream began. His subconscious had not had to reach into the future for material. Until maybe the end of the nightmare. A part of him might have been searching for answers then. What would he have seen if his mother hadn't woken him up? Alexa had been pulling off his gloves, and he had been removing hers. She had wanted it that way. She had wanted them to share their destiny, good or bad.

Herb reached over and blew a fleck of dust off his camera lens.

"I can be there in less than half an hour."

Herb reached into a drawer beside his workbench and removed a pocketknife. It was Swiss—strong, reliable. He pulled the blade free and felt the tip. Sharp as a razor, as they say. A half hour could be a long time in dangerous company. He searched for a place to hide the knife and finally decided to stash it under the pillow on his bed. He wasn't sure why he thought they would end up on the sheets. Probably just wishful thinking on his part.

Or maybe he had begun to recognize a pattern.

"I want to come, Herb."

Someone knocked at the front door.

Herb left his bedroom and stepped into the living room.

"Who is it?" he called.

"Alexa," came the sweet, feminine reply.

195

Herb opened the door. She looked beautiful, but then, he knew she would. She wore a loose-fitting red summer dress that barely grazed the tops of her knees. Her dark hair was down, long and tousled, as if she had just climbed out of bed to be with him. She smiled and showed off two rows of sparkling white teeth. In her right hand she carried a medium-size brown paper sack.

"Hello," she said. "What are you staring at?"

"Hi, Alexa," he said, stepping aside. "I've been waiting for you. Come in."

She peeked her head inside. "Is your mom home?"

"No."

She came all the way in, looking around. "Where is she?"

"Parvo."

"What's she doing there?"

"I think she went to see Theo."

"Have you talked to him?" Alexa asked.

"No."

"Have you talked to the police?"

"No. Would you like something to eat?"

"To drink." She held up her bag. Alexa had a thin face, perfectly sculpted. He could practically see her bones when she smiled again. "I brought something to eat," she said.

"What?" he asked.

"Cookies." Alexa opened the top of the bag and peered inside. "Courtesy of the Sugar Sisters."

Alexa made a face. "I don't mean that Lisa helped me make them. I made them myself—this morning." She added, "For you."

Herb moved toward the kitchen. "What would you like to drink?"

"Beer."

"Beer and cookies?"

Alexa followed a step behind him. "The breakfast of champions. Is something bothering you, Herb?"

Like maybe the bloody shootout last night? Or the burning cheerleader yesterday afternoon? Why should that bother me?

"No," he said. He took a beer from the icebox and handed it to Alexa. He removed a carton of milk for himself, and then sat at the kitchen table. Alexa sat across from him and pulled out a paper plate wrapped tight with tinfoil. Herb always liked tinfoil. It reminded him of picnics and airplanes. Alexa peeled it off carefully, revealing about two dozen chocolate-chip cookies. "They look good," he said.

"Thanks." Alexa popped the top off her beer and raised the can to her lips. "Have as many as you like." She grinned. "They're free."

"Would you like ice for your beer? A glass?"

"No, it's not as hot today."

"Not as hot as last night, you mean."

Alexa nodded. "Yeah, really. How did you sleep last night?"

"Like a dead man. How did you sleep?" She didn't look tired.

"Not bad."

"I had a dream we were both in."

"Tell me about it," she said.

"We were in the Old West. We were crossing the desert. We were out of water and our horses were about to die." Herb shrugged. "It was like a movie you might watch in the middle of the night."

"Was anyone else in it that we know?"

Herb thought a moment. "No. It was just you and me."

Alexa took another slug of her beer. "It doesn't sound very romantic." She picked up a cookie and handed it to him. "You must try them. I made them especially for you."

Herb just stared at the cookie. "You said that already."

"Did I? I'm sorry. They weren't any trouble, you know. Just something I threw together. I enjoy baking."

Herb chuckled to himself.

"What is it?" Alexa asked.

"I was just thinking that baking was a long way from acting."

Alexa smiled. "A girl needs something to fall back on in case things don't work out the way she plans. Don't you think?"

"Yeah." Herb took a bite of the cookie and chewed it slowly. He didn't taste anything unusual or suspicious. In fact he was surprised at how delicious the cookie was, like sugar and spice and everything nice. He turned back to Alexa, and marveled once again at how good she looked. That was the thing about beautiful girls—they always appeared fresh and new. As a photographer he knew that better than most. Alexa was exceptionally beautiful, and that must have been why he hadn't been able to capture the *real* her while shooting her portfolio. She had many faces she could put on, and it was next to impossible to sort them out.

"You wanted to protect Alexa."

He realized that he was in love with her.

Fitzsimmons had understood that immediately, God bless the man. Herb really would have liked to talk to him some more, but worried that it might never happen now. The reason wasn't completely dependent on how fast Fitzsimmons could drive. The sergeant was limited to knowing only what Herb would tell him. Herb was limited by what he was and what he wanted. He was a nobody who wanted somebody. He wanted the most beautiful girl in the world, and she was sitting only three feet away. She was his—for the moment—and he wanted to hold on to that moment as long as possible. It was silly, he knew, to cling to a few precious minutes when he had his whole life in front of him.

Yet none of this meant he wanted to die. He wasn't stupid. He realized his precious few minutes could last a deadly few seconds too long. Still, he didn't really know what was going to happen next. How could he? He had planted a camera and hidden a knife—all the tricks of the trade. But he was just playing the game.

I want to see if I'm as good at the game as she is.

Herb glanced at the clock. Fitzsimmons should be on his way. Then again, he might not be.

What else does she have in the bag?

Herb finished his cookie and reached for another.

"I'm glad to see you're enjoying them," Alexa said.

"They're great," Herb muttered. He drank his milk straight from the carton. It was good his mother wasn't there. She always yelled at him to use a glass.

"Will your mom be gone long?" Alexa asked.

"Long enough."

"What do you mean?"

Herb set the carton of milk down and smiled faintly. "I'm glad you came over. I've been thinking about you all morning."

She reached out and touched his hand. A fine white powder covered her fingers. She noticed him looking at them and quickly withdrew her hand to lick her fingers. "I often get sugar on me when I'm cooking," she said.

"You like sugar?"

"I like you." She finished sucking her fingers and reached for his hand again. "I wish we could have gotten to know each other under more pleasant circumstances."

Herb began to chew his second cookie. "It was the circumstances that brought us together."

"That's not true. We ate together before all this started." She batted her eyelashes. They were so long, so lush, anyone might have thought they were fake, but Herb knew they were real. If Alexa cast an illusion, it was from the inside. That was her strength. "I'm sure we would have become good friends if everyone was still alive," she said.

"But it would have been different," Herb said.

Alexa took another slug of beer and nodded. For a moment her gaze was far away. "It would have been a lot different," she whispered. But then she shook herself and turned her attention back to him. He could feel the power of it. Alexa was going to go a long way. She was hard to resist. He doubted that he could ever say no to her.

"What should we do now?" she asked.

"What would you like to do?"

She grinned, lowering her chin and raising her eyes like a little girl. "We could eat more cookies or—" Then she added shyly, "Or we could go in the bedroom."

"You haven't had a cookie yet."

His answer surprised her. He was talking about cookies and she was offering to sleep with him. "I'm not hungry," she said.

He finished his cookie and put another one in his mouth. They were fine. Everything was fine. He checked his watch. Soon his camera would begin to click. He would have to turn on his stereo to drown out the sound. He had another drink of milk.

"You're very pretty, you know that?" he said.

Alexa grabbed his hand. "Come on. Who are we fooling? Let's do it."

He stood up. He was surprised his heart was not thumping, as it usually did when he was excited or afraid. He actually felt quite calm as he nodded at the brown paper bag on the table.

"I hope you brought condoms or something," he said. "I don't have any."

Alexa let go of him and grabbed the bag, pressing it close to her chest. She acted embarrassed. "I've got *something*. You don't have to worry."

He grinned. "That's a relief."

They went in the bedroom. He didn't care this time that it was a mess. Alexa scanned the place closely before wrinkling her nose. "It smells like vinegar in here," she said.

"It's the developing solution." He sat on the bed. The smell had been there the previous night and she hadn't complained about it. "You get used to it."

Alexa stepped to the corner, to his makeshift darkroom. She picked up the roll of negatives that contained three other shots of naked Lisa washing her golden locks and scrubbing her face. "Do you have more of these?" Alexa asked.

"No," Herb said honestly.

Alexa set the negatives down and paused to take

a deep breath. Once more she stared off into the distance. Then she turned back to him. She set the brown paper bag on the floor near the end of the bed and sauntered toward him. She knew how to move her hips, looking sexy without looking cheap. She had style. She swung one leg over his and sat square on his lap with the grace of an angel.

"I love kissing," she said seriously.

So he kissed her, and this time he didn't hold his breath. He let himself sink deep into the sensation, feeling her wet mouth, her hot breath, as if they were a part of him. He began to understand why he had let Alexa run the show. He wasn't much different from her, not really. He ran his fingers through her hair now, and felt nerves deep in his brain wake up and groan with pleasure. Alexa leaned close to him and sighed.

"I want you so much," she whispered.

"Well, there's no one else waiting in line," he said.

She grinned at him and backed up slightly, her hair tickling his face. "You're naughty, you know that," she said.

"Boys will be boys."

Alexa stood suddenly. "Lie down."

"Are you going to lie down with me?"

"In a minute." She winked. "Afraid?"

"Can I put on some music?"

She stopped. "Huh?"

"I always like to make love to music." He shrugged like the cool dude he was pretending to be. "It's just a habit of mine. I hope you don't mind."

Alexa straightened her dress. Once more her eyes quickly scanned the room. Then she smiled. "I don't mind."

"Great." Herb stood and crossed to his stereo. It was in the corner opposite his darkroom. He didn't have a CD player yet—he poured any extra money he had into camera equipment—but his cassette player was of reasonable quality. Theo had a CD player and had recorded dozens of long-playing cassettes for him, with all his favorite songs. Herb's cassette player had a reverse switch. It would play both sides of the tape—a whole ninety minutes. Herb picked up a Led Zeppelin tape. It contained most of the band's first two albums. He slipped the cassette into the slot and twisted the volume dial up to six. He turned on the power.

Hard rock filled the room.

"Do you need it so loud?" Alexa asked, standing behind him near her brown bag.

Herb turned. "The louder the music is, the louder we can be."

Alexa chuckled. "All right, but don't blame me if the police show up at the door." She paused, a trace of concern darkening her sweet expression. "Are you sure you didn't talk to the police this morning?"

"Yeah. Why do you keep asking?"

"Because I tried to call you back and your line was busy for a long time."

"I left the phone off the hook after I spoke to you. I went back to sleep. That's when I had that dream I told you about." Herb climbed onto his bed and stretched out on his back. "It was very vivid."

"We were dying in the desert? It sounds like a nightmare."

"It depends on how you look at it. Roger Corbin was in the dream, too."

"I thought you said it was just the two of us?"

"It was. Roger wasn't really there. He was dead. The others were dead, too."

"What others?"

"Lisa and Sammie and Stephen. Oh, I'm sorry. Theo was there, too, and he was alive. He just had a little blood on his hands."

Alexa gave him a long grave look. "But we were alive?"

"Yeah. I think so. At least we were when I got woken up. I don't know, maybe we would have died if it had continued any longer."

Alexa continued to stare at him. "You have a rich imagination."

"That's what my mom always tells me."

"Is she going to talk to the police in Parvo?"

"Who knows what she'll do."

Alexa moved closer, till she was leaning her knees against the end of the bed. She reached down and squeezed his big toes through his socks. She squeezed them hard—she was a strong girl.

"We should get started," she said.

"I'm ready if you're ready."

She tossed her head, and her long hair curtained her face. She laughed. It was hard for Herb to hear over the music. Led Zeppelin had never sounded so fine. But Alexa's laugh was not so fine. It sounded strained.

"I want to tie you up," she said.

"Sounds dangerous. Should I take my clothes off first?"

Alexa shook her head. "That isn't necessary."

"Then will you take off your clothes?"

She lowered her head, and now her smile was pinched. Maybe she didn't like the music. Robert Plant was singing a sentimental song, a brief break from the heavy metal riffs. *"Babe, baby, baby, I'm going to leave you. . . . Leave you when the summer comes a-rolling."*

"It's more fun to wrestle with your clothes when there are things in your way," Alexa said. She reached down and took out a coil of rope from her brown bag. "Someone like you ought to be able to imagine that."

Herb smiled thinly. "I can. Very vividly."

He let her tie him at the ankles. She was quite good at it—he hardly felt the grip of the rope. His bed had no footboard. She had to stretch the rope under the bed and secure it to the legs. She had the end of the rope in hand as she approached the head of the bed and smiled down at him. His hands were resting on his chest, over his heart. He tried to hear what his beating heart was telling him now, but the music was an obstruction. Yet he did hear a faint click, just as the minute hand on his watch reached ten after twelve. Just a few minutes earlier he had synchronized his watch with the VCR.

Smile! You're on "Candid Camera"!

He only heard it because he knew it was coming. There was nothing to worry about.

Nothing to worry about?

"Are you comfortable?" she asked, reaching for his hands.

"Do you have to tie my hands?" he asked. It was an important question, a crucial moment. It was true she had his lower body immobilized, but with his hands free he could undo the rope in a minute. Unless she had another gun in her brown paper sack—the police had taken her revolver the previous night—he was still safe. But if she tied his hands in the way it appeared she was capable of, and he could not reach his knife, there would be no going back.

If I hold my hands at my neck when she ties them, there should still be enough play in the rope for me to reach under the pillow.

If—such a small word for such a big risk.

If he didn't let her tie him up, she might stop. She might just leave. Then there would be no incriminating pictures for the police.

Fitzsimmons should be halfway here by now if he's driving with the red light on.

"Are you afraid?" Alexa asked, and he could have sworn she was repeating herself from a minute ago. But that had always been a problem with him—his memory. Raising his eyes to Alexa, he was reminded of someone he could almost, but not quite, remember. A girl he had met somewhere, some time ago, under unpleasant circumstances.

"Are you?" he asked.

She sat beside him on the bed and put her free hand on top of his hands. "What are you thinking?" she asked.

He stared at the ceiling. "About the time I shot your portfolio."

"What about it?"

"I never caught the real you."

"What do you mean?"

"Everybody has an expression or a stance that says who they really are. They only show it occasionally. I never caught it in your shots."

"Does that bother you?" she asked.

"No. There's time." He turned his head in her direction. "Are you going to seduce me now?"

That was another thing that made him want to move to the next step. The possibility of sex. The possibility that all the deaths had been nothing more than horrible accidents.

Sure. Right. There's a good chance of that.

Still, she was so beautiful.

Alexa slowly nodded her head in response to his question. "Of course," she said. "That's what I'm here for."

He studied her eyes. They were bright, clear. The black spots he had noticed the previous night had vanished. Maybe he had only imagined them, like a bad dream.

"I believe you," he whispered.

She leaned closer. "I didn't hear you?"

He offered her his wrists—holding them near his throat. "Do it."

Alexa tied them. At first it wasn't so bad. His wrists were bound tight, but overall she had given him plenty of play with the rope. He could move his arms a foot in either direction. He could reach for his knife and be free in seconds, if necessary.

Alexa sat once more by his side. "How do you feel?" she asked.

"Vulnerable."

"With your clothes on?"

"You can take yours off now. I can't hurt you."

She nodded gravely. "If that's what you want." She leaned over and kissed him lightly on the lips. "Is that what you want, Herb?"

He thought about it a minute. Such a desire had been at the root of the madness. At least, his share of the madness. There was more than one madness at work here. If he hadn't set up the camera and VCR, Lisa would probably still have gone flying and landed in a heap of smoking ashes. He shook his head.

"I'd rather talk," he said.

"About what?"

"All the things we couldn't talk about when my hands were free."

Alex drew in a sharp breath. It was as if all the smiles and laughter she had put on the last two days were suddenly wiped clean. They had all been faked. There was nothing but cruel pain left now. It was only when Herb saw this pain exposed that he fully realized Alexa Close was capable of anything.

Including murder.

"You know," she said finally.

"Yeah, I guess. But I don't know everything. How did you do it?"

"Do you really want me to tell you?"

He shrugged as best he could. "Yeah. I'm not going anywhere. It'll help me pass the time."

She smiled. "You're funny."

"Thank you."

Alexa stood and walked over to his darkroom, specifically his workbench. She leaned back against it, not far from the peekaboo lens of his camera. He thought he had just heard it click for the third time, but he couldn't be sure. It would make sense, though. He had set the program at five-minute intervals. He doubted she could hear it click. With the music on loud, she'd have to be listening for it specifically.

"Can I lower the music?" she asked.

"I love this album. It's one of my favorites."

She wasn't suspicious. "All right, have it your way." She paused. "Where should I begin?"

"At the beginning."

"I'd rather not tell you about my childhood."

"You don't have to. You've told me enough of that already. Why don't you begin with Roger Corbin."

"Ah." She nodded. "He's a good place to start. Lisa and I liked him."

"Both of you?"

"Yeah, Lisa and I were great friends. We shared everything, including our boyfriends. Does that shock you?"

"How far did you share them?"

"All the way. We only did things all the way. That's the only way we could have any fun in this town." Alexa stopped and chuckled. "Roger was a blast. He was such a nice guy when we got ahold of him. It took a lot of effort to mold him to our liking. Do you know how we did that, Herb?"

"You turned him on to cocaine?"

"That's correct. Coke and sex. We were always sweet to our boys. The nickname Sugar Sisters suited us perfectly. We kept our habits private, except to a select few males. Roger was one of those, and he was one of the best. It took us a while to get him addicted to the drugs that is. He took to Lisa and me right off. But Roger didn't like putting things in his body. He was into being healthy. That side of him was boring. We had to practically *spoon*-feed him. But after a while he loosened up. Then he was of use to us."

"At getting you more drugs?"

"Yeah, you know the sweetest things in life are always the most expensive. Lisa and I, we were proper young ladies. We couldn't break into houses and steal things because we were too short to reach the windows. But you remember what a hunk Roger was? After we had him trained, he used to bring us all sorts of goodies. Then we'd take them, and sell them, and buy other kinds of goodies."

"I've heard this story before, on TV."

Alexa laughed. "I suppose, but no one on TV or anywhere in the world did it as smoothly as we did. We knew how to make a boy eat candy out of our hands."

"Why did you do it?"

"It was fun. It was something to do until I got to L.A."

"You were addicted. You're addicted now."

Alexa lost her smile and her eyes turned cold. "I can control myself. I can control any situation. I don't need your lectures."

"Excuse me. It seems you lost control of Roger."

Alexa shook her head in disgust. "That was Lisa's fault. Roger was complaining that he hated stealing. He wanted to stop. Pangs of conscience— they bother every good boy eventually. All we had to do was soothe him for a couple of weeks and he'd have come around. But Lisa wanted to give him shock treatment. We invited him up into the hills and tied him up between two trees."

"We?"

"I showed up a little later. I decided if Lisa wanted to shock him, then we'd better shock him good. Lisa had several grams of coke with her. She taped Roger's mouth shut and held the coke right under his nostrils. Whenever he breathed, he had to snort coke. You see how that can be, can't you?"

"Yeah." He could picture it with remarkable clarity. "How did Lisa get Roger to agree to being tied up?"

"She probably told him some delicious lie. Boys love to be lied to." Alexa paused to think. "Anyway, we were going to do all sorts of fine things to him, and convince him that he really didn't want to go against the Sugar Sisters and lose all his fringe benefits, but he just kept getting angrier. I'd never seen him so mad. Lisa might have fed him too much coke. Other than that there was no way to explain his superhuman strength. He actually snapped one of the ropes that tied him to a tree. Then there was no stopping him. He began to undo the other ropes, and we knew that if he caught us he might hurt us. We ran toward my car with Roger tearing after us. We barely got away from him. But he had his car nearby and he got in it and the chase was on. I tell you, he was foaming at the mouth. Our two cars were doing an easy ninety miles an hour down the hill, and you know how that road winds. I was driving. When we got to the turn at the cliff, I had to swing wide. I couldn't keep the car in the right lane. Unfortunately a car was coming up the hill at that exact moment."

"Sammie?"

Alexa nodded. "Sammie. When she saw Lisa and me heading toward her, she swerved onto the shoulder. But she swerved too hard and almost went off the cliff. It's a shame she didn't in a way. She tried compensating, I think, by yanking the wheel in the other direction. She went into a spin and ended up in the middle of the road. By this time Lisa and I were past her. But Roger was coming around the turn, and when he saw Sammie, he did everything he could to avoid her. But she had both lanes completely blocked. There was nowhere for Roger to go." Alexa shrugged. "So he went off the side of the cliff."

"And that was the end of Roger?"

"Yeah. Poor guy. But it was just the beginning of our problems. Lisa and I parked and jumped out and ran back to Sammie. We figured she'd seen our car and could identify us later. But Sammie must have been daydreaming when we almost hit her. She thought the accident was her fault, although she did know Lisa had been speeding. That's right, she thought Lisa had been driving. Don't ask me why since we were in my car. Anyway, we hurried to the edge and looked down. Roger's car was an inferno. Lisa immediately started crying. She was such a great actress. She started screaming at Sammie that Sammie had killed her boyfriend."

"Wasn't Lisa genuinely upset?"

"I suppose she could have been. But she wasn't that attached to Roger, if you know what I mean."

"He was just a *boy.*"

"Yeah," Alexa continued, without noting his sarcasm. "But he was someone who could get us into serious trouble, even though he was dead. I took Lisa aside and spoke to her for a few minutes. We couldn't let Sammie talk to the police, we decided. We had left tire tracks halfway down the hill. Tracks like that can be traced to a particular vehicle, especially when the authorities would have had only two vehicles to examine. We knew if someone examined the tracks in detail, they would know what had happened. Also, we were high as the moon. We had so much coke charging through our bloodstreams, we were practically bouncing out of our shoes. We knew we'd be spotted by the police and our condition would be tied to the drugs in Roger's system. We decided the best thing to do was just get in our cars and get the hell out of there, and pretend we'd been far away when Roger died. Of course Sammie went for the plan. It saved her tail as well. Lisa and I promised her we'd never tell a soul. We cooked up the story of the movie we supposedly went to in Parvo."

"It sounds like you covered every base."

Alexa shook her head, "Every base except human nature. As time went on, Lisa began to kid me about how I murdered Roger. She would say it just in a joking way, but I knew Lisa. I knew her jokes were more dangerous than most people's threats. Then there was Sammie. As the months passed, and she had more time to think about how fast we were driving, and where she was when she swerved onto the shoulder, and where we must have been to force her to do so, she started to figure out that she wasn't entirely at fault. She came to me and told me that she wanted Lisa and me to admit we were also responsible. She didn't say she was going to the police, but the idea of it was always hanging in the air between us. You can see how it was—both of them were picking at me from both sides. And I didn't like it, not one bit." Alexa stopped. "Then Lisa tried to poison me."

"Are you serious?"

"Yeah. By this time we had Stephen working for us. He wasn't as much fun as Roger. He was stupid, but he had a body, and a car, and he didn't mind dirty work, as long as he was compensated. Lisa took a pile of jewelry Stephen had stolen to San Francisco to hock so that she could buy the coke. It was the first time Lisa ever went. I usually took care of that end of the business—alone. I had all the contacts, and I didn't trust her or Stephen with the money. But I was sick that weekend, and Lisa wanted to go, and I was curious to see what she'd do with so much junk, if she'd steal it or what. We're talking about three grand worth of saleable goods here."

"Stephen would just swipe the stuff and turn it over to you?"

"He might have kept some things for himself. But he never kept much, I know that. He was afraid we'd hand him over to the police."

"Sounds like a wonderful relationship."

"I told you I didn't care for him," Alexa said.

"I never realized how little. Go on." Herb

wanted her to go on. He wanted her to talk and talk. Time was his only friend, besides the knife under his pillow. He flexed his wrists, his hands. If he rolled on his side, he should have no trouble getting the knife. And Fitzsimmons was on his way.

You know, buddy, he didn't exactly say he was coming.

"This trip of Lisa's took place two weeks ago," Alexa continued. "I called ahead and told my people she was coming. On the jewelry end of the deal she did just what I told her, but when she went to buy the coke, she got it from someone I didn't know. And this person gave her bad stuff along with good stuff. And Lisa gave me the bad stuff, but I didn't know how bad it was until I stuck my face in it and snorted a noseful."

"What did it have in it?"

"I don't know. It could have been strychnine. Pushers often use it to add a kick to their product when it's been diluted with sugar or baking powder. It's a powerful stimulant even in small doses, and it's very dangerous. I went into shock after trying it. My nose bled at least a quart. I could have died. The autopsy on Stephen will tell what was in the crap."

"You gave the stuff to Stephen?"

"Not until yesterday. But after Lisa returned from her shopping trip and gave me the poison, I told her I didn't want her sharing any of her supply with Stephen. I wanted to make Stephen angry with Lisa. But Lisa agreed to my request readily. She had probably finished half her coke before she got back to Mannville. Lisa had a real nose for it. In fact, she was already into freebasing and crack. I never touched that stuff."

How conservative of you.

"Wasn't Lisa surprised when you didn't die?" Herb asked. Her story was fascinating, in a sick way. Even more amazing was the way she told it in a perfectly normal tone of voice.

"Yeah, she must have been," Alexa said. "But she hid it well. And what could she say? 'Sorry I tried to poison you.'"

"How do you know her coke wasn't contaminated as well?"

"She was the one who bought it. She would have told me. No, she was trying to get rid of me." Alexa paused to look out the window. She seemed distracted and frowned. She added, "You can see why I had to kill her."

"And Sammie?"

Alexa waved her hand, dismissing both him and Sammie. "They both had to go. They were both a danger to me. Sooner or later they could have joined forces and blamed Roger's accident on me. I had no choice. I began to make plans. I thought the way Roger had died was neat: the dangerous turn; the body burned to bits; the lack of any evidence. I was convinced a hard blow to the head could be easily explained by a fall off a cliff and a gasoline tank explosion. I also enjoyed the irony of the whole idea—wasting Lisa and Sammie in the spot where it had all begun. But the more I thought about it, the more I realized I couldn't knock Sammie unconscious until I had Lisa safely out of it and at the top of the cliff."

"You needed Sammie's help?"

"Yeah. I needed her to drive up the cliff behind me. I couldn't hitchhike away from the scene of the crime. I also needed Sammie to help me carry Lisa out to her car, or, as it turned out, Stephen's car."

"What was Lisa doing with his car?" Herb asked.

"That was just a coincidence. Hers was in the shop. She borrowed it from him. I told him to give it to her. I didn't want to make her suspicious."

"Was Stephen in on this plan?"

"No."

"But why didn't you use him instead of Sammie? It would have been safer for you." Herb realized then that it must have been Sammie who had come to the school in the middle of the night to make sure he had rigged the camera.

"I'd already had enough experience with things from the past coming back to haunt me. I didn't want to bring in a third party. I wanted to close the book on the matter myself, and have no witnesses that I'd just have to kill later. Besides, Stephen wasn't a killer, not really."

"Sammie wasn't either. How did you convince her to help you?"

"I went to her privately and told her Lisa was preparing to hand her over to the police for the death of Roger. Sammie freaked. It took me forever to calm her down so I could speak to her. But finally she was ready to do anything I told her."

"I don't believe it," Herb said. "She wouldn't have helped you kill Lisa."

"She didn't have to kill her. I told her I'd do that. She just had to back me up. It was a reasonable proposition. I'd take care of the dirty work and she could live worry-free for the rest of her life. Sammie's eyes lit up when I told her my plan. She hated Lisa's guts."

"Maybe Sammie's eyes lit up because she had a plan of her own."

"Ain't that the truth. I was plotting to put Sammie in the car with Lisa, and Sammie was plotting to put me behind bars. I underestimated her and that was a serious mistake. I take it she went to you at this point and talked you into rigging your camera in the girls' showers?"

"You knew all along it was me who took the pictures?"

"Of course. Do you think I'm an idiot?"

"No," Herb said thoughtfully. "You're not that."

"I also knew she couldn't have told you everything about what was going on because you would have gone to the police. Am I correct?"

"Yeah. I was out in the cold."

"You just wanted some kinky pictures, huh?"

"Yeah."

Alexa smiled and continued, "Sammie didn't trust me at all. She insisted she had to have a gun in case Lisa got loose or something dumb like that.

Sammie must have suspected I wanted to take her out as well. But I was suspicious of her. I did agree to supply her with a gun, but I watched her closely from the day I told her about my plan till the day we carried it out. Like any guilty person, she did make a mistake. Last week, out of the blue, she made an off-the-wall comment about what if a picture of us braining Lisa ended up on the front page of the newspaper. Her voice accidentally cracked as she said it, and I asked her what she was talking about. She began to fidget and stutter and deny that she meant anything. But it made me wonder. I thought to myself, Sammie knows exactly when we are going to commit the nasty deed. Is it possible she could frame me, and still let me go ahead with the murder? I thought about it a long time. Then I bumped into you Thursday afternoon—Sammie's old friend, the best photographer in the school. Something clicked. I began to wonder what Sammie had planned, and if you were involved."

"You were nice to me because you were suspicious of me?" Herb asked, hurt. The illusion that the most beautiful girl in the school might like him just faded, leaving only a void. Only one thing gave him any satisfaction now: hearing the camera click for the fourth time. Alexa had obviously heard nothing.

"I enjoyed your company, Herb," Alexa said. "It doesn't matter that I wanted something from you. You wanted something from me. That's just the way it is."

"I didn't want anything from you."

"You wanted a nude picture of me. I don't mind, all's fair in love and war." She stopped. "Do you want me to go on?"

"I want you to untie my hands and feet."

"I can't do that. Not after what I've told you."

Herb snorted. "Then go on. Tell me the rest."

"I studied you closely. But I couldn't draw any direct link between what Sammie and I were going to do and you. You seemed too nice to get mixed up in it. I was reassured, somewhat, but I still had my eyes open. Then Friday afternoon arrived."

"Why did it have to be that Friday?"

"It didn't. It could have been the next Friday, or the one after that. Fridays were good, though, because we practiced our full routine, and usually took showers afterward. Lisa and I never showered before the other girls left. We liked to get stoned before we got under the water. There's nothing like a hot shower when you're high on coke."

"Do any of the other girls on the squad have your habit?"

"No."

"Why did you have to kill Lisa in the shower?"

"I didn't *have* to kill her in the shower. If I did, fine, but I wasn't going to bash her over the head an extra ten times to make sure she was dead. But I did have to hit her in the shower."

"Why?"

"Because of the blood."

Herb grimaced. "Did she bleed a lot?"

"Oh, yeah. It poured down the drain like a river."
Alexa paused. "Friday afternoon arrived and
Sammie was nervous. I admit I was scared myself.
Sammie still insisted she had to have a gun. I
couldn't talk her out of it, so I gave her one of my
dad's pistols. It takes a six-shot clip. I loaded it with
blanks, except for the top bullet. I had to make that
one real."

"Why?"

"Because I thought Sammie would check the
clip, but I doubted that she'd check all the cham-
bers. Giving her the gun didn't scare me as much as
you might think. I couldn't see her putting it to the
back of my head and blowing my brains out. Too
much evidence. She would just go to jail. Sammie
was terrified of jail."

"It sounds like you were, too."

Alexa nodded. "I feel like I've been in jail all my
life, living in this town. I told you that in McDonald's. I can't stand walls, real or psychological ones.
That's why I couldn't bear the threat Lisa and
Sammie held over my head. But let me finish.
Friday afternoon at four o'clock Lisa was soaping
herself in the shower. I waited until the other girls
on the squad left and then I went to meet Sammie
at the door of the showers. I gave her a gun and told
her to wait by the equipment cage, near the mirror.
By the way, that's how I spotted her so quickly in
your photograph. I knew she was there."

"Did you have another gun with you?"

"Yeah, the revolver. But I had it hidden out of

sight under my shirt. Sammie didn't know I was armed, too. I grabbed a bat from the equipment cage and told Sammie to stay put until I returned. She was shaking so badly her teeth were chattering. As I walked toward the showers, I could hear the water running and Lisa singing. We had just snorted a couple of lines a few minutes before she got in the shower so she was feeling good. And you want to know something—I felt pretty damn good myself."

"You enjoyed killing her?"

Alexa's eyes shone with a dark light. The black specks were back, swimming around the wide-open dilated pupils. Herb realized Alexa was stoned right then.

"Lisa turned as I stepped into the shower," Alexa said. "She looked at the bat and asked me what I was doing with it. I didn't say a thing. I just raised the bat over my head. Then she knew what I was doing with it. She took a quick step back and threw up her arms to protect herself. She didn't scream, though, I've got to hand her that. She was tough. But she stepped back too quickly. She slipped and fell to her knees. Her arms came down as she tried to regain her balance. She just knelt right in front of me, kind of like a sacrifice. I brought the bat down on her head quickly. The wood cracked—so did her skull. She fell facedown on the tiles, with the water streaming on her back. The blood—"

"Don't tell me about the blood!" Herb interrupted.

"The blood gushed over her blond hair. It was

much darker than I thought it would be. It pumped out, in rhythm to her heartbeat. But then it began to slow down. The water washed it away, and her hair turned nice and clean again. She stopped breathing. I thought she was dead."

"She wasn't?"

"I'll get to that. I went back and fetched Sammie. I'll never forget what she did when she saw Lisa lying naked on the tile floor. Her face broke into a wide grin, and then she vomited. We had to use the showers to wash that mess away, too. We got a couple of towels and dried Lisa off. We had to dress her, you know. It would look suspicious that she had driven off the cliff stark naked. I had to put on most of her clothes because Sammie was of no help. All she did was tie the laces on Lisa's tennis shoes."

"This is gross," Herb said.

"It gets better. I drove the Fiat onto the lawn right beside the showers. We carried Lisa out to it. She weighed more than I would have guessed, but then dead people are funny that way. Sammie gave me a hand getting her into the front seat of the Fiat."

"Why didn't you put her in the trunk?"

"We tried. She didn't fit. I wasn't worried about driving around with her seated beside me. I had her propped up pretty good. I even put on her sunglasses. She didn't look too bad."

"Oh, swell."

"I drove up to the cliff. Sammie followed me. We parked on the side of the road near the ledge. There was no one around. I still had the baseball bat with me. Sammie noticed it as she walked up to the Fiat. She demanded to know why I had brought it. Her hand was on the gun in her pocket. She was freaking out. I had a time calming her down. I told her I had just brought the bat because I didn't want the murder weapon lying around. I explained to you a minute ago that the bat cracked when I walloped Lisa, but I only realized at the cliff that it was going to be of no use to me in killing Sammie. My plan wasn't perfect. I don't think any murder plan could be. So I decided the hell with it—I'll kill Sammie later. I had Sammie help me move Lisa into the driver's seat. It was then that Lisa started to come around."

"God."

"Sammie was fastening Lisa's seat belt—Lisa always wore her seat belt—when Lisa groaned. Sammie almost fainted. She fell back on the ground and wet her pants all the way through. It would have been hilarious if we weren't in such a dangerous predicament. I still had to get the Fiat over the cliff, and I knew I couldn't just roll it over. I knew the police would expect the car to fly some distance from the ledge, if it had any velocity at all. That was the hardest part of my plan. On TV, people drive cars to the edge of cliffs and then jump out at the last second. That's all B.S. I wasn't going to risk my life doing that. Besides, Lisa had to be behind the steering wheel."

"What did you do?"

"I had thought about it earlier. I had a wooden stick with me that I had measured well. I planned to jam it between the seat and the accelerator. If the car exploded on impact—and I thought that it would—the stick would burn up and the evidence would disappear. It was a narrow stick. If the car didn't explode, I planned to hike down to the bottom of the gorge and remove the stick."

"That would have taken time and been risky."

"With Sammie dead or out cold, yes. I may not have even used the stick if I'd already clobbered Sammie. But Sammie was still helping me. She could have just driven off, and when I had the stick, I could have disappeared into the gorge if people came."

"How were you able to maneuver the car with Lisa groaning in the driver's seat?"

"It wasn't easy. She was waking up more with each passing second. I had to squeeze in beside her. She had started bleeding again and she was drooling on her blouse. She muttered my name, and something about cookies."

"Why did you two bake those cookies?" Herb asked.

"For money for drugs. I thought that was obvious?"

"I suppose. Did they have cocaine in them?"

"Just a tiny bit. Gave them a special flavor. Anyway, Lisa was mumbling to me about another bake sale and I was trying to back the car into the road so that I could give it a running start. When I had the Fiat where I wanted it, I wedged the stick in. The car just took off on me. I hardly had a chance to slam the door shut. It drove straight for the edge. Lisa must have been totally awake then because she sat up straight. You could see she was frantic. She started screaming even before the car plunged over the cliff."

"That's sick."

"That's the way it happened. The car exploded on impact as I had hoped. It was loud. Sammie and I took one quick look at the fireball and got in her car and split. We drove back to the school. We took the bumpy road you and I took in case anyone was coming up the road. That had been probably my biggest worry—that someone would drive by while we were dumping the Fiat over the edge. But you know that road. Few people take it any time of the day. Still, we did luck out."

"Why did you have to go back to the school?" Herb asked.

"To get my car."

"Why did you both drive back to the cliff?"

"It was natural that *I* should go that way—it was on the way home. Sammie wasn't supposed to come. But then, she was already making a pain of herself."

"In what way?"

"She was acting cocky, like we had pulled it off but she still had my number. I didn't like it. It made me even more convinced that something was going on that I didn't know about. She wouldn't give me my gun back. I couldn't exactly wrestle her for it. She followed me back to the cliff. I could see her in my rearview mirror smiling."

"She knew you had been photographed clobbering Lisa."

"Obviously. But she hadn't let her scam out of the closet yet. I drove by the scene of the accident and stopped to see what the problem was. When I saw it was my best friend, I acted crushed. I think I did a wonderful job acting."

"Why did you tell me on the ride to Parvo that Lisa was a coke freak?"

"Why not? It was going to come out anyway."

"Why did you have me give you a ride?"

"Because I enjoy your company."

Herb wasn't smiling. "Seriously."

"Because I still thought you might be the key to what Sammie was up to. But I couldn't approach you directly, not yet. I was the grieving friend. There had been no opportunity for me to become aware of a frameup, not yet, not from your point of view. I was hoping you would offer some clues, though. When you didn't, I decided to have Sammie drive me back from the police station."

"You waited at the station to hear what the autopsy revealed because you were worried about the blow to her head?"

"Exactly. I wanted to see if they believed the accident had caused it."

"They wouldn't have told you if they thought it hadn't."

"I would have been able to tell. What was that cop's name?"

"Fitzsimmons."

"He didn't seem that bright."

"He might be smarter than you think."

Alexa's eyes narrowed. "What's that supposed to mean?"

"Nothing."

"Were you talking to him this morning?"

Herb checked the clock by his bed. Thirty minutes had elapsed since he finished talking to Fitzsimmons.

He should be in Mannville by now.

Then again, Fitzsimmons might still be in Parvo.

"Maybe," Herb answered.

"Tell me." -

"No."

Alexa glared at him for a moment, then she relaxed. "You're just trying to get me worried so I'll let you go."

"Sure, that's it. Did Sammie tear into you in the car?"

"Yeah. We had hardly left the police station when she started giggling about how she had pictures of everything that had happened in the showers. I was shocked. I didn't know how she could have managed it. No one else had been in the showers, I was sure of that. I wondered if she was bluffing, then dismissed it. She was so sure of herself. I realized a camera with a timer hooked to it must have been set in the showers. I also realized Sammie was too much of a klutz to do it, so my attention returned to you. I called you after Sammie dropped me back at my car at the cliff."

"Your car was still at the cliff?"

"Yeah," Alexa said. "I had to go home to call so Sammie got to your house just when I got to my phone."

"There was no note?"

"Of course not. I typed it up just in case you did have pictures. When you admitted that you did, I got scared. I had to think fast. I had to use all my skills to get my hands on those pictures before Sammie did."

"You used the fact that I liked you," Herb said bitterly.

"Don't take it personally. I was cornered. You said Sammie was at the door. I told you to get rid of her and call me back immediately. When you didn't, I called Stephen. I ordered him to go to your house and get the pictures, no matter what. I might have overreacted. Stephen must have arrived there just when you were leaving to come to my house. That's why he had to chase after you in Lisa's car."

"Where did he get Lisa's car?"

"The shop, I guess. The repairs must have been finished. What's the matter? Did you think you had a ghost on your tail?"

"No."

Alexa chuckled again. "I think you did. You were white as a ghost when you got to my house."

"What did Theo have to do with any of this?"

"Nothing so far, not from my side. I didn't have Stephen call him till later. I'll get to that. When you reached my house and told me what had happened, I realized I'd made another mistake. I asked you how many prints you made, but I forgot to tell you to bring the negative. I thought if I got my hands on that, and Stephen had the only print, I'd be in good shape. Yet the more I thought about it, the more convinced I became that I had to get rid of Sammie immediately. It was clear she was against me. Even if her scheme was falling apart, she had brought everything out into the open. But without her around, I knew her accusations would just dry up. I began to plan how I could get rid of Sammie and Stephen both."

"Why Stephen?"

"Because he had seen the picture. Besides, he was becoming a pain in the ass. I'd wanted to get rid of him for some time."

"When and why did you give Stephen the contaminated coke?"

"I gave it to him Friday morning. I was half hoping that he'd be dead by the afternoon. But he had a strong system. He loved the junk! He thought it was the best he'd ever snorted. Can you believe it? It gave him the most incredible bloody noses and he didn't even care. He was totally strung out all day Friday. I could have given him a machine gun and told him to go down to the mall in Parvo and take out as many people as he could, and he would have done it."

"I thought you said he wasn't a killer at heart."

Alexa shrugged. "That was when his blood wasn't boiling over with cocaine and strychnine. Now where were we? Oh, yeah, we were driving to your house. When we got there, your mom said Sammie was going to call back, so I decided to bide my time. The negative was in the next room. I decided to see what Sammie did before choosing a counterattack. Then Theo called. I remembered what you said about him shooting at Stephen. That impressed me. I also remembered how bitter he felt about his brother's death. It was then, and only then, that I figured out how to tie all the loose ends together."

"Did you call Stephen when you went back into my house to use the bathroom?"

Alexa nodded in the direction of the door that led directly from his bedroom to the bathroom. "Yeah, I couldn't wait till we got to my house. I needed Stephen to have already contacted Theo by the time I reached home, in case I had to devise an alternative strategy. How did you know I called him?"

"I don't remember hearing the toilet flush." Herb coughed. His throat was dry. He would have liked a glass of water but didn't want to ask for one. "You gave Stephen instructions to bait Sammie about what happened to Roger. You were just trying to provoke Sammie to shoot Stephen, and Theo to shoot Sammie. There never was a package."

"I told Stephen that Sammie had stolen a package of coke that belonged to us. I also told Stephen to bring a knife. I didn't think Stephen's verbal threats would be enough to get Sammie to pull out her gun. I took Stephen's knife away before the police arrived and hid it. I wanted to make Sammie appear more unstable than she was. But otherwise you are correct with your guesses."

"How come the gun didn't scare Stephen?"

"I told him ahead of time that Sammie would be armed, but that she didn't know her gun was full of blanks."

Herb shook his head. "You just sent him to his death, when he hadn't done anything to you."

Anger flashed in her voice. "So what? He would have tried to hurt me eventually. He was a guy. All guys are the same."

"You'd know, I guess."

"What's that supposed to mean?"

"I was just thinking of poor daddy and his crippled legs."

Alexa waved her hand again. "That happened a couple of years ago. He got what he deserved."

"What did you do to him?"

Alexa grinned a secret grin. "Nothing I didn't enjoy."

"I'm sure." Herb measured the play of the ropes again. He was going to have to move for the knife soon. He couldn't wait for Fitzsimmons. "Are you through?"

"Except for a few small points. You realize there

was no danger of Sammie killing me when I charged her. She was firing blanks at that point. But when it was all over, I had to get rid of the blanks in her clip. They would have made the police suspicious. You notice how I insisted we hike down to the bottom of the gorge and check on Sammie before the police arrived?"

"Yeah." At the time Herb had strongly resisted what he thought was an altruistic gesture on Alexa's part. He knew there was no help for Sammie. He didn't want to see what was left of her, but see it he did. The fear he had expressed to Theo on the hill had come true. The jagged point of the wreckage had practically pierced Sammie in two. The charred metal had still been dripping dark drops of blood as they approached. Sammie's open eyes were wide with staring horror.

"Now you know everything," Alexa said. She took a step toward Herb. Her face was difficult to read, but he knew he wasn't seeing anger. A portion of her earlier sorrow had returned, and now it was mixed with puzzlement. "Now you must tell me something," she said.

"What?"

"Why did you let me tie you up? You knew when I got here that I was behind it all."

Herb sighed. Led Zeppelin was still going strong on the speakers on his right. But he'd already heard a faint click between Jimmy Page's heavy riffs. Number four was in the bank. "I've been asking myself that same question," he said.

Alexa sat on the bed beside him. She touched the ropes on his left wrist, and the flesh beneath them. She caressed his hand gently. "Do they hurt?" she asked.

"Not too much." He added, "I don't think they're going to leave any marks, unless I start working on it now."

"Don't."

"Why not? What have I got to lose?"

"What have you got to gain?"

"Nothing."

"You didn't answer my question. Why did you let me tie you up?"

"I just wanted to see what it felt like to be tied up by a pretty girl."

"Seriously," she said.

Herb looked at her beautiful face and felt the pain of a lifetime. A lifetime of watching and never acting. He realized there was a chance he was going to die in a few minutes, and he had never even asked a girl out on a date.

"I am being serious," he said, and he wasn't totally lying. He was trying to set Alexa up, true, as she had set them all up, but he had hoped it had been for nothing. Now he had no hope, except to stay alive and put her in jail.

"I don't understand." And it was clear that she *did* want to understand, this twisted psychopath of a girl. Herb couldn't comprehend that. Everything she told him indicated she had no feelings for him, or anybody for that matter. She was an ice statue, beautiful but deadly. Herb moistened his lips with his tongue. They were parched, as if he had just marched across a barren desert.

"You have always been a fantasy of mine," he said, again being more truthful than his secret knife and his secret camera would have had people believe. "Then when we started talking on Thursday, the fantasy suddenly became real to me. Something I could reach out and touch. Then all the craziness started, and I just wanted to touch you all the more. But the picture fell in my lap, and I looked at it, and I studied it, but I don't think I ever saw it. It was too real. It was the *real* you. I had finally caught Alexa Close on film. Do you understand?"

"The reality was too much for you?"

"Yeah."

"And you denied to yourself that I was the killer?"

"I think so."

"But you weren't denying it today when I arrived. You talked to someone."

"Yeah. Fitzsimmons."

Alexa paused. "What does he know?"

"Everything."

"He knows I killed Lisa?"

"Yeah. And he knows you're responsible for Sammie and Stephen, too."

Alexa cocked her head to one side, regarding him closely. "You wouldn't be saying these things just to get me to let you go?"

"That's for me to know and you to find out."

She spoke decisively. "It doesn't matter what you told Fitzsimmons. Without the picture and the negative, he has no proof. And I burned both of those last night." She let go of his hand and put her palm over his heart. "All Fitzsimmons has is your testimony. Soon he won't have even that."

"You're going to kill me?"

"I don't want to," she said.

"But you have to?"

"Yes."

Herb sniffed. It was embarrassing—he suddenly felt like crying. He just couldn't take bad news. Of course, this was *very* bad news. "I'll tell you why I let you tie me up if you promise to let me go," he said half in jest.

"I'm afraid I can't make that kind of deal." Alexa brought her face close to his. He could see every detail in it. All the colors and tones and lines that came together and made magic in his mind. But he saw something else, something from the past. A face glimpsed on a dark and dangerous night. The night of the water balloons. That was it. Long dark hair caught in a blast of orange gunfire. The girl in the Porsche.

It was she who had had the gun, not the guy.

It was Alexa Close.

Big deal. She's done far worse since then.

But it was a big deal. She had tried to kill them for an innocent prank. She was that kind of monster.

238

"Why did you let me tie you up?" she asked for the third time, and this time Herb heard suspicion in her voice, cold and definite.

Go for the knife! Go for the knife! Fitzsimmons isn't coming!

"Because I'm an idiot," he said.

Alexa drew back, her eyes still on him. "I don't believe you."

She knows I'm up to something.

Herb went for the knife.

The move did not go as well as he planned. First, the knots around his ankles were tighter than the ones around his wrists. As he started to roll over, he got stuck halfway. Second, while hiding the knife, he had positioned it with the handle at the top of the bed, not toward the bottom, which would have made it much easier to grab. Still, the knife was only a couple of inches beneath his head and he did have the play in his arms. Even in his half-stuck position, he was able to scoot the pillow out of the way and reach for the knife. Alexa had drawn back at a favorable moment. He could see he was going to get to the knife before her.

He reached up with his sweaty fingers.

He grabbed the blade.

Behind him, off to his side, Alexa moved in a blur of speed.

Herb began to turn the blade around.

I'm going to beat you!

Not quite.

Herb felt a terrible yank.

His hands were snapped down.

The knife flew from his fingers and fell on the floor.

Alexa bent over and picked it up. She had the rope in her hand. It was one continuous piece of rope. He had forgotten that small point. She had yanked on the other end. She was smiling. Yet her eyes were strangely flat. He imagined that was the way they had looked when she had stuck it to her old man.

"That was close," she said.

Alexa tossed the knife aside and knelt beside her brown paper sack and drew out a roll of gray duct tape and a Baggie partially filled with snow-white powder.

"I assume you know what this is?" she asked.

Well, you blew that one, buddy.

Herb glanced once more at the clock.

"I can be there in about half an hour. I want to come, Herb."

It had been more than half an hour. A lot more.

"Sugar," Herb said bitterly. He hadn't wanted the photos to turn out this incriminating. He realized she was going to kill him.

"Yes," Alexa said. She set the Baggie down on the side of the bed, leaving both her hands free to handle the tape. "Sugar and salt."

Once more, Alexa moved quickly. Before Herb could fully comprehend what she was up to, she had ripped off a piece of duct tape and was descending on him.

She's going to gag me.

Herb twisted his head frantically to the right, to the left, but her hands were stronger than his neck muscles, and now his wrists were pulled tight and there wasn't an inch of play in his arms. She grabbed him and held him still. He fought her as best he could, but it was hopeless. He spat in her face just before she sealed his lips.

"Roger did the same thing to Lisa," she remarked, calmly wiping away the saliva. She pulled the tape tight, and then, in a more leisurely manner, added a second piece on top of it to keep him from screaming.

She's really going to do it.

Alexa reached for her Baggie of white powder. She poured a small amount into her palm. She was sitting at a good angle as far as the camera was concerned. The lens would capture them both perfectly. The real Alexa Close.

The real Herb Trasker. The fool.

Herb thought back to what Theo had said that night at work, about them always being failures. The way things had turned out, Theo had been right. Yet more than anything else, Herb wished Theo was with him now, so that he could tell his best friend that it didn't have to be this way. Suddenly Herb felt that he could have been someone. That he could have been great.

It was a strange thought for a dead man to have.

"I like your shirt," she said. "I wish I could tuck a napkin in your collar so the blood won't ruin it. But the police would wonder about it when they find you overdosed on bad medicine." She raised an eyebrow when she saw how big his eyes had become at the mention of blood. He had never cared for it, especially when it was his own. It made him want to throw up. Yet if he did that, he knew he would smother.

But that might be better. More evidence. I could go out like a rock star.

His choices were just wonderful.

"I didn't mean to scare you," she said. "It won't hurt too much, as long as you cooperate. Don't be like Roger was when Lisa spoon-fed him. He kept yanking his head from side to side. He wasted a lot of coke that way. Granted this stuff is laced with strychnine, but maybe the poison can be filtered out of it later. I don't want to waste more than I have to." She caught herself and made an apologetic face. "I'm sorry. You can't be worrying about my supply at a time like this. You have to die." Alexa moved her palm toward his nostrils. "Just be easy, and I'll let you die softly," she promised.

Herb immediately yanked his head to the side. This time she grabbed him by the hair. She was incredibly strong for a cheerleader. Her grip was more like that of a football player. He fought her again, squirming every direction his muscles would allow, but it was like the episode with the tape. Soon he tired and couldn't resist any longer. She yanked his head with her right hand, yanking out clots of hair in the process. She reached for her

Baggie with her left hand. The first lot of powder had already spilled on her. She poured a second dose and moved it close to his nostrils.

"You can hold your breath if you want," she said. "But you won't be able to hold it long. The powder's very fine. When you inhale, it will enter your system. There's no escape. There never was. I could tell from the start you'd do what I wanted. Boys always do, except when they're bad. Don't be a bad boy, Herb. I honestly do like you. I don't want you to have to suffer unnecessarily."

Alexa shoved the powder in her left palm directly under his nostrils. Herb held his breath. He counted to ten. His heart began to race. He counted to thirty. His heart began to scream. He counted all the foolish things he had done in the last couple of days and by then he had reached a hundred and his heart was ready to burst. Alexa waited for him. She was patient. She waited for him to count past a hundred and fifty. At that excruciating point he was forced to draw in a desperate breath through his packed nostrils.

"That's a boy," she said, patting him on the back.

The powder immediately clogged his nasal passages; there was too much of it. He had to suck in a number of short frantic breaths to get any oxygen down into his lungs. Finally the powder began to dissolve somewhat, but as it did, it burned. He felt as if someone had rammed a blowtorch high into his sinus cavities and turned on a blue flame. The pain was more than he could have imagined. He snorted out as hard as he could, trying to dispel the powder, but all he succeeded in doing was spraying the front of his shirt with blood.

"I know the feeling," Alexa said sympathetically.

Through the drone of the music, and the pounding of his heart in his ears, Herb thought he heard the camera click once more. For all he knew Alexa would still be around for the eighth shot. She would have cleaning up to do. She could be in every shot, and they could pin the prints on his tombstone. Fitzsimmons could blow them up and use them for wallpaper. Herb just hoped to God the cop found them in time. Before Alexa killed again.

And this Herb realized was inevitable.

The drug began to enter his brain. It didn't promise him a smooth ride. He immediately began to hallucinate. Alexa's pupils turned solid black. He blinked, trying to clear his vision, and she blinked back at him and the whites of her eyes turned black as well. They were now wide-open windows into her soul, a starless void, where not a trace of light shone. She grinned a mouth filled with glowing teeth, her lips so red they looked as if they dripped blood.

"That wasn't so bad, was it?" she said—and reached for more powder.

EPILOGUE

The small California town of Mannville had had its heart torn out. When kids died before their parents, it wasn't right. It wasn't the natural progression. That's what the local paper said, and that was how the people felt. The mothers and fathers of the dead hadn't begun to comprehend the immensity of their loss. They turned to one another for solace and asked why. *Why?* No one had an answer. They held all the funerals on the same day. The funerals for Lisa Barnscull, Stephen Plead, Sammie Smith, and Herb Trasker.

Alexa Close stood in the cemetery by the freshly dug graves, her head bowed low. The minister was rambling on about the kingdom of heaven and the valley of the shadow of death and other nonsense. He was giving her a headache, but it wasn't difficult for her to keep a straight face. It was an absolute requirement. She had supposedly lost more than any of the other kids at school, and everyone was watching her. She gave them a good show—a tear here, a shudder of weakness there. She was a wonderful actress and knew that the same people who stood in mourning around the graves would be reading about her in movie columns soon. She was going to be a star. It was her destiny.

Goodbye, Lisa. Goodbye, Sammie. Goodbye, Stephen. Be sure to write!

Goodbye to you, too, Herb, Alexa thought. He had been more fun than the rest of them combined. It was a pity he had never gotten to see a nude picture of her. Had it been possible, she would have had one taken and pinned to his grave marker. She was sure he would have enjoyed the irony of the gesture.

The service ended finally. Alexa waited in line to hug each of the dead kids' parents. They all squeezed her tightly when she reached the front of the line, especially Herb's mother. She was such a nice woman. It was a shame that life could be such a bitch at times.

Alexa turned to leave the cemetery. She had her father with her, the smelly old goat. Her mother was at home with a barbiturate hangover. Alexa took hold of the bars at the back of her father's wheelchair and eased him away from the graves. What she would have loved, though, was to dump him in one of the holes and shovel dirt on his face. He deserved it, the way he had tried to teach her about boys before she was ready to learn. But there was always time for a premature burial, before she left for L.A.

What a fine way to say goodbye to a difficult upbringing.

Herb Trasker's mother was ahead of Alexa on the narrow stone path that led out of the cemetery. Alexa was surprised to see that the woman had not waited in line to hug everybody. Alexa was even more surprised to see that Mrs. Trasker had been *called* away from the line by a police officer. Alexa recognized the man—Sergeant Fitzsimmons. He was shuffling a handful of photographs in front of Mrs. Trasker's eyes. He was talking excitedly and pointing.

Is he pointing at little old me?

He was. He waved for her to come over. Alexa whispered to her father that she'd be a moment and walked toward the policeman and Herb's mother. Alexa wasn't sure what was going on, but the hollow calm she kept secure inside her was suddenly invaded by an annoying buzz. She didn't like the buzz. She preferred the emptiness, always had. Mrs. Trasker was glaring at her. Alexa came to a halt a few feet in front of both of them.

"Did you want me?" she asked pleasantly.

Mrs. Trasker struck her in the face. The blow amazed Alexa, as did the blood that gushed from her nose onto the black silk blouse that she had bought especially for the funerals. She was reminded of all the coke she had snorted in the last year and of Herb. He had bled a lot before she had finished with him. This must have something to do with him.

Dammit! Him and his goddamn camera.

Mrs. Trasker spit in Alexa's face and stalked away. Sergeant Fitzsimmons took Alexa by the arm. His grip was firm, almost painful. He handed her the photographs to look at.

"You are a wicked girl," he said flatly.

Alexa glanced at the top picture. Herb was lying tied to his bed. His shirt was soaked red. She was sitting beside, feeling at his neck for his pulse, smiling. It was not a flattering picture. The camera lens had caught her poor side. Herb was dead, of course. She had left him that way. Suddenly she wished she could join him. She knew she wasn't going to get out of this one.

"At least I'm not a wicked boy," she replied.

Fitzsimmons read Alexa her rights.

Look for Christopher Pike's

Bury Me Deep

About the Author

Christopher Pike was born in Brooklyn, New York, but grew up in Los Angeles, where he lives to this day. Prior to becoming a writer, he worked in a factory, painted houses, and programmed computers. His hobbies include astronomy, meditating, running, playing with his nieces and nephews, and making sure his books are prominently displayed in local bookstores. He is the author of *Last Act, Spellbound, Gimme a Kiss, Remember Me, Scavenger Hunt, Final Friends* 1, 2, and 3, *Fall into Darkness, See You Later,* ~~Witch~~, all available from Pocket Books. *Slumber Party, Weekend, Chain Letter, The Tachyon Web,* and *Sati*—an adult novel about a very unusual lady—are also by Mr. Pike.